BURY THE HATCHET

By Tim M. Dutton

Bury The Hatchet

Copyright © 2011 by Tim Dutton

http://warriorcombatives.com/

ISBN: 978-0-9840839-1-6

Published in the United States of America

Table of Contents

Chapter 1
Nightmares Turn to Dreams

1864 Virginia...

A bloody Civil War battlefield, you can tell this used to be a beautiful Country hill side, but now it has been ravaged by war. Bodies of both men and horses are strewn about, trees have been uprooted and explosions have created craters in the ground.

The sounds are deafening, gunshots, explosions, screams and other battle field sounds can be heard all around. The stench is stifling the smell of gunpowder, smoke, sweat, blood and death linger in the air. There are two opposing forces doing battle here today, the North and the South.

The forces for the north are a Dragoon. The term dragoon literally means "mounted infantry." Infantry were trained to fight on the ground.

Calvary were trained to fight from horseback. Dragoons were trained to fight from any position. Dragoons were the elite forces during the Civil War. The forces for the South are a group of Confederate Partisan Rangers. Partisan Rangers were highly trained and experienced volunteers. They were not payed a commission like enlisted men, instead they were payed with bounties. These were men who truly believed in what they were fighting for and were prepared to give all for god and country.

Cole Hawkins, a Confederate Partisan Ranger, in his late twenties, stands with a rifle in his hand, he sees a Yankee Dragoon soldier on horseback using a saber to cut down fellow Rebel Partisan Rangers, who are standing on the ground.

The Yankee slashes downward into one of the Ranger's shoulder.

The Ranger falls to the ground in pain, bleeding from his wound. The Yankee then stabs another Ranger in the neck, who falls, he's dead before hitting the ground. The Yankee then turns his attention to a third Ranger.

Cole aims and Fires his rifle. The bullet strikes the Yankee in the chest, Falling from his horse, his body hits the ground and he does not move.

The Ranger looks at Cole and nods as to thank him. From behind, a second Yankee Stabs The Ranger in the Back with a bayoneted rifle. The Yankee stands over the body of The Ranger, he spots Cole and in a screaming rage, he charges on foot at Cole with a bayoneted rifle.

Cole narrowly parries the attack and sticks his

own bayonet deep into the Yankee's midsection, pushing him all the way to the ground.

Cole pulls his bayonet free from the now lifeless body and spots, Captain Kendall Brody, a Union Dragoon Captain, who is slightly older than Cole.

Kendall, on horse back charges at Cole with a Saber held out at his side. As Kendall approaches Cole, an explosion between the two opponents knocks Cole, Kendall and the horse to the ground.

Cole slowly stands temporarily deaf from the explosion. Cole watches, in silence, as Kendall's horse stands. The horse staggers for a moment, gets it's footing, looks around and bolts away.

As Cole regains his senses, sound returns, and he can hear once more. Cole turns his head to see Kendall. Kendall crawls toward a revolver, grabs the revolver, aims and fires, felling a Confederate Partisan Ranger.

Cole urgently looks to both sides for a firearm of any type but sees none. Kendall still lying on the ground takes aim again and shoots another Ranger, who slumps grabs his gut and falls to his knees.

Cole wastes no time pulling his knife as he sprints toward Kendall. As Cole reaches him, he grabs Kendall's hair and pulls back his head.

Watching from a distance is Colonel Munroe Brody, a young Dragoon Colonel for the Union army and Kendall's older brother. Munroe is wounded and unable to move. Munroe reaches toward Kendall and screams. "KENDALL LOOK OUT. STAY AWAY FROM HIM YOU DAMN DIRTY REB. NOOOOO."

Cole cuts Kendall's throat.

1874 Kansas...

Cole Hawkins, abruptly sits up in bed, drenched in sweat and breathing heavy. He is now in his late thirties, with a muscular build. It was a nightmare, but it was still real it happened ten years ago. From all the things he did in the war, this is what he has nightmares about. The same one for all these years, lived over and over.

Tara Hawkins, Cole's wife is in her late twenties and is slender with slight functional muscularity. She sits up next to Cole and touches him tenderly. She knows whats wrong, it's been happening ever since they married six years ago. She knows her husband well and knows he will shut down if she forces the issue. So she goes through the motions and eases into it. "Cole? What is it?"

"Nothing. I didn't mean to wake ya. Try to go back to sleep." Cole says as he turns his head toward Tara and kisses her on the cheek, then turns to face forward again in heavy thought.

"Was it the war again?" Tara asks.

Cole responds with a simple "Yea."

Tara inquires farther "Same dream?"

Once again, lost in deep thought Cole responds with a simple "Yea."

Tara reaches up and gently, grabs Cole's chin and turns his head toward her. "Look at me. You always close up, after you dream about this, like your trying to hide some deep, dark secret or something. Maybe it would help if you talked about it."

4

Ashamed Cole turns his head, so he doesn't have to look Tara in the eyes. "No! I don't want you to know about that part of my life."

Tara knows this can't go on, she will have to push the issue this time. "A husband and wife shouldn't keep secrets from one another."

Cole continues to look straight ahead and does not acknowledge what Tara just said.

Tara continues "You carry this like a heavy burden, but its not just pulling you down, it's also pulling you away, away from me and Sara."

This is enough to get Cole's attention "I don't want it to."

Tara gently places her hand on Cole's shoulder and pleads "Then please open up to me Cole. Just like any other weight, burdens are easier to manage when you have help. Share this with me and I know, together we can carry it through."

Cole, with sad eyes, turns to face Tara. "If I tell you what I done in the war..." Cole ducks his head, unable to finish his statement.

"What?" Tara asks.

Cole doesn't answer.

Tara tries again "What will happen if you you tell me?"

Cole hesitantly responds "You'll think I'm a monster and you'll hate me for it."

Tara smiles warmly. "No Cole. Look at me. I may not have fought in any wars, but I'm also not some naive little girl, who's been sheltered from the world. I know that good men must sometimes do bad things in order to get by or survive and its even more so in war or when they go up against bad men."

Cole responds with "Still don't make it right."

Tara continues to try to reassure her husband. "Some things are beyond right and wrong. I know the man I married is not a monster. I can't promise you that I won't be surprised, saddened or even disappointed at times. What I can promise you is that nothing you ever say or do could ever make me hate you. I love you Cole Hawkins and that's forever." "Now the question is, are you going to trust me enough to share your burden?"

Cole, already in better spirits, looks directly into Tara's eyes. "I love you too and I trust you with my life and more. So, if you want to know, I'll tell ya, everything, every last bit of it."

And he does, He tells her every detail. He tells her about the killing, the scrounging for food and ammo even off of dead bodies from both sides. He tells her about things no one should ever have to do.

Tara listens and as she Promised she's shocked and surprised at times, but she never judges Cole and she still loves him. Also as Tara promised, Cole feels as though the weight of the burden he's carried for so long is a bit lighter now. He has new hope, the burdens of war feel as though they are manageable now.

They say war is hell. Cole Hawkins believes he has just escaped from his hell. He still carries some quilt, but he knows with his wife by his side it will get better everyday.

Four weeks later...

Hawkins ranch is not big and it is definitely nothing fancy or extravagant. It is just a small ranch with a house, a barn and some corrals containing mustangs. For Cole, Tara and their little girl Sara, it's enough.

Cole leans against a corral watching his daughter play in the dirt.

Sara Hawkins, Cole and Tara's daughter is four years old and is a petite little tomboy. She is trying to dig a hole in the dirt with a shovel that is bigger than she is. Her clothes are smeared with dirt where she has wiped her dirty hands. Her face also has smudges where she tried to wipe sweat off her face and out of her eyes. She continues to dig with youthful vigor. Whatever she is digging, she's determined to get it done.

"That shovel is bigger than you are sweet pea." Tara says, as she walks past Sara toward Cole.

Sara still determined responds. "I can handle it mama."

Tara smiles proudly and says " I never doubted it for a second."

Cole smiles as he listens to his wife and daughter's conversation.

As Tara approaches Cole, she asks "Did you get the chores finished?"

Cole nods his head once affirmatively and responds with a "Yes ma'am."

Tara wraps her arms around Cole's waist, Cole gently gives Tara a quick kiss. "Supper's ready, now that you let your daughter get all filthy." Tara says

7

jokingly.

Smiling Cole responds "Oh! She's my daughter when she's filthy uh?"

Tara turns around to face Sara, her back to Cole, but still with his arms wrapped around her, holding her close. "Nah, filthy or not I won't deny her." Tara proudly states, then asks "Whats she doing anyway?"

Cole shrugs his shoulders "I don't know. You know how independent she is, she had to do it herself. Knowing her curiosity and lack of fear, she's probably trying to dig to the devil, just to see what he looks like, or to beat him with that big shovel of hers."

Tara laughs and says "I wouldn't doubt it one bit."

Cole squeezes Tara a little tighter and says "She's a rough and tumble tomboy, just like her mama.

Tara smiles "There ain't no prim and proper, sissified, Miss prisses around here. You want to trade us off for some fancy Nancy?"

Cole is quick to answer "Heck no. I'll take my rough and tumble girls over anybody, any day." "What about you, you ever wonder what it would be like to have some dandified gentleman slicker pampering you all day?"

Tara answers "Nope. Like I said I ain't no prim and proper, sissified, Miss priss." She smiles and slyly looks up at Cole and says "I don't need no pampering, you'll have to do for now."

Cole knows she's being playful and he's ready. "I'll have to do? For now? I'll show you how I do."

Cole starts to tickle Tara on both of her sides.

Tara pulls away and tries to cover her sides. "Stop it." Tara can barely get the words out for laughing.

Cole wraps his arms around Tara and holds her close, he looks up and sees Sara smiling as she watches. "You're next little Missy." says Cole.

Sara smiles and shakes her head back and forth. "No I'm not!"

Cole raises his eyebrows and nods his head up and down affirming his statement.

"You've been in a lot better mood lately and I like it." Tara says.

Cole loosens his grip and Tara turns around to face him. She continues "You also haven't jolted me awake in the middle of the night for almost four weeks now."

Cole smiles at her and says "I haven't been having nightmares about the war. Ever since I opened up to ya, it's like I was finally able to bury my past and move on. I guess if ya can stay with me after knowing, then like it or not I can except what I done and put it behind me. You were right."

"I was right?" Tara asks, then trying to keep a straight face she states "I'm always right. There's a well known rule that states all wife's are always right and husbands should listen and obey.

Cole counters with "Listen and obey uh? How about instead I..."

Chapter 2
Introduction of Evil

Cole stops talking, the smile on his face is replaced with a worried look. He steps back from Tara and looks toward the barn, then he looks toward the house. His time in the war taught him to pay attention to all of his senses and have given him very good survival instincts. He knows something is wrong. He can't see it, but he knows something or someone is here and he can almost sense the negative intentions.

Behind the barn...
Stand eight men on horseback, all of them dressed in faded Dragoon uniforms. The only difference in Calvary uniforms and Dragoon uniforms was the braiding, Calvary had yellow

braiding and dragoon had orange. These are eight of the thirteen men calling themselves the *Hatchet*.

The one in front is Colonel Munroe Brody, a big, burly, well dressed Dragoon Colonel,in his late forties. This is the same man that watched Cole kill his brother during the war. He's a capable leader, but the war has made him just a *little off* in the head. Munroe is holding up a fist in the *hold position* posture.

Behind the Colonel is John " J.T." Trevor, the youngest member of the hatchet, he has a slender build and is neat and clean shaven.

The rest are bunched together and include, Buck Weston, the Hatchet's scout, he is lean and muscular and wears traditional Union dragoon uniform except he wears a red breech-cloth over is trousers, a red bandanna as a headband and moccasins instead of boots.

Lieutenant Wade Brooks, who is very fit and neat in appearance.

Clay Dawson, who is normal and average looking in every way.

Emmett Boggs, a heavy set, very mean and angry looking man in his forties, with a rough complexion, an eye patch and a scar that runs diagonal across his face from under the eye patch, past the edge of his nose and to the corner of his mouth. The hairy mole on his nose is his most attractive feature.

Avery "Tenderfoot" Bennett, is a skinny man with glasses, he looks more like a *tenderfoot* than a member of a Calvary or Dragoon.

The eighth horseman is Leroy "Preacher" Dobbs, a Tall lanky, bible toting, hypocrite. He is also the oldest member of the Hatchet.

The eight men are trying to hold position quietly, as to not alert their prey.

Behind the Hawkins' house...

Stands four men on horse back, the two on each end are brothers. On the right is Sergeant Jack Farley, he has an average build, is neat in appearance and is the older brother of Jake.

On the left, Corporal Jake Farley, Jack's younger brother, he is also neat in appearance. Both men wear faded dragoon uniforms, with highly polished sabers. It is visually obvious that both the brothers take great pride in their sabers.

the two men in the center are Tyson "Ty" Parnell, a scrawny, slouchy man who has a cocky look about him and

Charley "Red" McBride, a stocky, flaming red headed Irishman with a temper to match.

In the far distance...

On a hill behind the house there is a wagon stopped and waiting. The man in the wagon is Zeke "Skinner" Hoyt, heavy set, dirty, filthy and disgusting. His Union uniform is ragged, slouchy and blood stained were he has wiped his hands. His scraggly and wiry beard has dried tobacco spit in it and there's a leather thong of human ears hanging from his pistol belt.

In front of the house...

Cole is still looking around as though he knows someone is close and up to no good.

Concerned Tara asks "What is it?"

"Get Sara and get in the house." Cole urgently replies.

Fearful Tara tries to inquire further "What...",

But is cut short By Cole's worried Shout "NOW TARA! GET IN THE HOUSE!" Cole draws his revolver and continues to look back and forth from the barn to the house.

Tara, now realizing something is definitely wrong, runs over to Sara, picks her up and starts to run toward the house.

"Whats wrong mama?" Sara asks sensing something is wrong.

"It's going to be okay sweet pea." Tara says.

Before Tara can reach the house, Jack and Jake on horseback ride around opposite ends of the house and meet at the entrance, blocking Tara's path.

"What's the hurry ma'am? Why don't you stay an visit with the rest of us?" Jack asks with an arrogant tone.

Cole points his revolver at Jack and cocks the hammer. "Let my wife through, then you can state your business, and you best be quick about it."

Before anyone can respond Cole hears the sound of horses behind him. Then he hears the sound of lever action rifles being levered and revolvers being cocked. Then he hears the surly voice of Munroe.

"That's not very hospitable, Mr. Hawkins. Now, lower that pistol and try to be a little more friendly.

We wouldn't want those pretty little ladies to get caught in the cross fire, now would we?"

Cole slowly releases the hammer on his revolver and re-holsters it. Cole turns to see the eight horseman from behind the barn. Some of the men have rifles and some have revolvers, all of them are pointed at Cole and his family, Munroe, empty handed is the closest. "Have we met?" Cole asks.

Munroe responds. "We've never actually danced but we've been on the same battle field."

Cole is fearful for his family and is becoming agitated "Who the hell are ya an what do ya want?" Cole asks, in a noticeably angry tone.

Munroe leans slightly back and sarcastically responds " Well now, that don't sound very friendly, but what the hell, I'll introduce our asses anyhow." Munroe places his hand to his chest arrogantly. "I am Colonel Munroe Brody." Munroe takes his hand off his chest.

The rest of the men relax their weapons.

Munroe continues "As for these other mean son's of bitches." Munroe nudges his head up towards J.T., who in return nods at Cole. Munroe continues his introduction. "That's John Trevor, but we just call him J.T."

Cole now very irritated speaks up. "I don't need ta know all of yer names. What do ya want?"

The men of the Hatchet quickly raise their weapons back up and point them at Cole and his family.

Munroe looks back at Cole, with a mean hateful look. It's the kind of stare that sends shivers down

14

your back. Munroe calms himself, relaxes his features and posture and addresses the Hatchet. "Easy, men. Easy."

The Hatchet, once again relax their weapons.

Munroe clears his throat and turns his attention back to Cole. "I'm getting ta that, so shut up and listen. I want you to know everyone of us, before we get down to business." Munroe points to Buck, who winks and makes a kissing face at Tara.

Cole steps in front of Tara to block Buck's view.

Munroe smiles and says "That there is Buck Weston he's our scout, ain't nothing or nobody he can't track." Munroe points to Wade,

Wade tips his hat. "This one here is Lieutenant Wade Brooks. He is now my second in command and he is a very capable man." Munroe now points at Clay,

who just smiles. "Clay Dawson, there's nothing special about him. No offense Clay."

In an average and dull voice Clay responds. "None taken, Colonel."

Munroe continues "Although, he's loyal and gets his job done." Munroe is taking his time. It's intentional, he's trying to stall long enough for the two men in back to gain access to the house.

Inside the house...

Ty and Red are now trying to climb through a back window.

Ty falls through the window and onto the floor. He whispers his complaint. "Damn it! That hurts, we always get the shit jobs."

15

Red looks through the window to make sure Ty is out of the way, then starts climbing through the window. He is not having any easier time getting through the window, he falls to the floor with a THUD.

"Be quiet, ya big oaf." Ty whispers.

Red quick to anger responds in a loud voice. "I'M TRYING..."

Ty slaps his hand over Red's mouth to keep him quiet. "Shut Up. You don't have to get so loud you damn, angry bastard. You're going to have to control your temper before they hear us." Ty whispers.

Red is still pissed, but lowers his voice to a whisper, or at least an angry whisper. "Fine! I said I was trying and you didn't do any damn better, asshole."

Ty responds with his own angry whisper "Whatever. We're in now, I don't think anyone heard us, we're fine."

In front of the house...

Munroe continues his introductions and points at Emmett.

Emmett just scowls at Cole.

"Emmett Boggs, There ain't no one more experienced in combat than that man there. He can kill a man with one hand while he's wiping his ass with the other." Munroe moves his pointing finger to Tenderfoot,

who sits up nice and straight, like a proud peacock.

"That's Avery Bennett, but we call him

16

Tenderfoot because... well on account of him looking like a tenderfoot. But don't let them looks fool ya, there's nothing tender about that bastard." Munroe points to Preacher,

Preacher holds his bible out.

"The old man there is Leroy Dobbs, but we just call him Preacher, cause he's always tot'in that bible around. He believes if he hides behind it his sins won't stick."

Preacher holds his bible up and says "The good book is my shield, God will forgive any sin if ye but ask..."

Munroe interrupts "Yea! Yea! We don't wanna hear another one of your God Damn sermons. I'm talking here." Munroe shakes his head and rolls his eyes in disgust, as he looks back at Cole. "He used to be a Chaplain, now he's just another god damn killer like the rest of us."

Munroe brings his pointing hand to his face, looks at it and wiggles his finger and then shakes out his hand. "That there's a lot of damn pointing. Oh well, we're almost done."

He's still stalling to make sure Ty and Red have enough time to get in the house. Munroe raises his other hand with index out, shows it to Cole and smiles smugly. He then points toward Jack and Jake Farley. "You've already met the Farley brothers, ya just ain't been formally introduced. The one on the right is Sergeant Jack Farley, the one on the left is Corporal Jake Farley. We sometimes refer to them as the Saber Brothers, on account of their fondness for those sabers. They'd rather kill a man with a saber than any other weapon."

Jack draws his saber and points the tip at Cole. "There's nothing more satisfying than cutting a man down with three feet of cold steel." Jack says.

Munroe smiles and says "Now put that away Sergeant. You're scaring our host."

Jack, without saying a word and still looking at Cole, licks the blade of his saber, then re-sheathes it.

The sound of a wagon rapidly approaching gets everyone's attention.

In the distance...

Skinner is bringing the wagon in fast and hard. "HAW! HAW! GET GOING YOU NAGS!" yells Skinner as he furiously whips the reins. The wagon kicks up dust behind it as it roars down the dirt trail by the house.

Ty and Red signaled Skinner when they breached the house.

Now skinner is on his way to tell Munroe.

In front of the house...

Munroe motions toward the wagon. "Aah! Last and probably the least too, coming in the wagon is Zeke Hoyt. We call him Skinner on account of... well we won't get into the why of that right now." Munroe tilts his head back and takes a big sniff of air, lets it out, then looks back at Cole. "Take a whiff, you can can likely smell him from here."

As Skinner nears...

He slows the wagon and pulls up close to the rest

of the Hatchet and stops, by pulling hard on the reins. "WHOA, YOU FILTHY NAGS!" Skinner bellows. Skinner looks at Cole, spits tobacco juice on the ground, then looks at Munroe. "It's time Colonel." says Skinner.

Munroe responds "Fine, just fine. Now take the wagon on out about another mile or two and wait on us there."

Skinner is eager to obey. "Yes sir, Colonel." Skinner looks forward and yet again slaps the reins hard and bellows. "HAW! HAW! YOU HEARD THE COLONEL! GET GOING YOU NAGS! HAW! HAW!"

The wagon bolts forward and starts kicking up dust again as it continues on it's way.

Munroe turns his attention back to Cole and says "Well that's just about everybody, give or take."

Cole is angry and responds "Can't say I'm pleased to meet ya. Ya still haven't told me why the hell yore here."

Munroe sarcastically adds "You need some patience, Cole. Can I call ya Cole? Course I can, we all know each other real well now."

Preacher chimes in with a sermon type tone "Patience is a virtue, virtue is..."

"SHUT THE HELL UP! Don't interrupt me again." Munroe says. Munroe closes his eyes, tilts his head back, takes a deep breath and slowly lets it out, in order to calm himself. He then opens his eyes and looks at Cole Once more. "Now then, where was I? Oh that's right. We call ourselves the Hatchet. We chose that name because our sole purpose in life is to chop off the limbs of the confederacy and believe me, we're damn good at it."

Chapter 3
The Nightmares Return

Cole, in a slight state of surprise, looks at Munroe. Cole then shakes his head back and forth in confusion. "THE WARS OVER!... It's been over for nearly ten years. What are ya some senile old bastard, that likes to dress up and play war? Hell! I reckon the lot of ya are crazier than a bunch of shit house rats. Then again I reckon saying that is disrespectful to the rats."

Munroe sarcastically looks at Cole "First rudeness and poor manners and now insults, your hurting my feelings Cole." Munroe gets a more serious look on his face and continues "Besides, crazy or not, the war ain't over for us and it won't be until every last God damn Johnny Reb is dead and buried."

Still a bit confused Cole asks "So, you're just going to go around killing every ex-confederate soldier you can find?"

Munroe gets a cocky look about him and responds. "You bet your britches we are, but not just kill'em, we're going to torture'em and not just ex-rebs neither, but anyone who fraternizes with'em too. All southerners and their sympathizers are nothing but scum and need to be disposed of."

Munroe slowly rides his horse closer to Cole. "You Cole Hawkins are the worst one of all, you killed my brother. We're gonna treat you extra special."

Cole slightly turns his head as though he's trying to remember. Then he realizes his nightmares have come back to haunt him. Only this time they are made of flesh and blood and have come to drag him back to hell. "Kendal Brody?"

Munroe looks like he's offended that Cole even uttered the name. "Yes, that's right, Captain Kendal Brody. I knew you would remember the man you murdered in cold blood."

"IT WERN'T MURDER!" Cole is quick to respond, then he calms down and continues. "I was a soldier in a war. I'm sorry about your brother, I truly am. It even haunted me for a time, but I was doing my duty, I killed him to prevent him from killing other soldiers. I'm sorry for your loss, but you need to take your men and get off my land."

"HELL NO!" Munroe yells, he is now thoroughly pissed. "You don't give the orders, here. Duty? Duty my ass, we don't recognize the duty of

22

rebel murderers." Munroe composes himself and reverts back to sarcasm. "However, we're not complete cold blooded killers."

The men of the Hatchet snicker and laugh.

"That's a good one, Colonel." Buck says.

Munroe smiles a kind of crooked smile and says "Okay. Ya got me, we are, but we can still be fair. We'll give ya a nice, fair trial right here." Munroe looks around at the Hatchet. "All you scum sucking bastards that think Cole Hawkins is innocent, say innocent and put a bullet in your own head."

There is no response. Every member of the Hatchet is still and quiet.

Munroe continues with his so called trial. "Now, everyone who believes this murdering Rebel bastard is guilty, say guilty."

The men of the Hatchet look at each other and smile and slightly out of unison, respond. "GUILTY!"

Preacher chimes in and adds a little extra. "GUILTY AS HELL!"

Munroe looks back at Cole and leans towards him from the saddle. "Looks like your one guilty son of a bitch. I knew you were and now it's been proven in a court of law. I sentence you to be tortured to death." Munroe proudly leans back into his saddle.

Cole looks at him with an angry look, a stare that seems like it could burn a hole clean through him. "Yea, that's one proper ass trial there, Judge Shit for brains."

Munroe smiles and says "I thought ya might like

it."

Cole knows there is no reasoning with this man, but maybe there's still hope for his wife and daughter. "There's nothing I can say or do that's going to change yore mind. So, do what you will with me, but leave my wife and daughter out of it. They had nothing to do with any of it."

"They're with you ain't they?" Munroe says.

Cole now truly pissed, takes a step toward Munroe.

The hatchet immediately point their weapons at him.

Munroe a little afraid raises his hands, palms facing Cole and says "Whoa! Calm down."

Cole, still pissed stops to hear him out. Cole knows he can't take them all and Tara's and Sara's life depend on these men sparing them.

Munroe looks up and can see through a front window, he sees Red standing in the house looking out.

Red casually salutes to Munroe through the window, then turns and walks out of sight.

Munroe smiles and looks back at Cole. Munroe would like Cole to know what he plans to do to his family, but he knows Cole would fight with every fiber of his being. Munroe also knows that even though They could kill Cole, there's a good chance that Cole could take a few of them with him. Munroe considers it might even be himself. He's not willing to take that chance. So he decides to air on the side of caution and see if he can get Cole to submit willingly.

"I'm not completely heartless."

The men of the Hatchet relax their weapons and laugh yet again.

Munroe smiles and says "Okay, you got me again, but here's what I been thinking. You were a Partisan Ranger under the command of Colonel Mosby, who we liked to call the Gray Ghost, on account of every time we thought we had that bastard, he'd just up and disappear on us."

Chapter 4
A Deal With the Devil

Cole calms and relaxes a bit, he hopes to hear something that makes sense.

Munroe continues. "So, anyway that means your one highly trained son of a bitch, and there's no doubt in my mind that even though we could kill ya, you could probably take a few of us with ya. So, for that reason I'm will'in to make you a deal."

Cole slightly nods and says "I'm listen'in."

Munroe lays out the deal. "It's like this, you cooperate and do everything I say and we spare the woman and child" "Hell! Who knows you cooperate and you might just survive this yourself. We got a deal?"

Cole nods his head in agreement.

Munroe puts his hand behind his ear as though

he is listening. "I know your a man of your word Cole, I got to hear you say it."

Cole is reluctant, but he knows it's his family's only chance. "Deal."

Tara is shocked. "NO! You can't just do what they say Cole. They'll kill you anyway."

Cole walks over to Tara, who is still holding their daughter tightly in her arms. Cole grabs Tara by the shoulders and pulls her close and softly says "I have to do what is going to be the safest for my family."

Tara fights back tears and shakes her head side to side. "No, Cole. Whats best for your family is having you here with us. There's got to be another way."

Cole tries to console his wife. "Shh, listen to me, there's no other way. You have to take care of Sara, she's all that matters now. I love you both more than anything."

Tara doesn't like it one bit, but she knows Cole is right. This is Sara's only chance. Tara looks Cole in the eyes and with tears running down her cheeks says "I love you too."

Sara now sobbing says "I love you, Pa."

Cole fights back his own tears, kisses Tara, then kisses Sara. He wraps his arms around both of them and squeezes tight. He knows this may be the last time he gets to hold them. He let's go, steps back and still fighting back tears, smiles and says "Get in the house."

Jack and Jake both look at Munroe for approval. Munroe nods once in agreement.

Jack and Jake back their horses away from each

other creating a gap.

Tara carries her daughter between the two horses and into the house.

After Tara has entered the house Cole turns back towards Munroe and says "Let's get it over with."

Munroe pleased with himself smugly smiles. "That's fine by me. First I want you to drop that holster on the ground. Then I want you to get on your hands and knees an crawl, That way." Munroe points in the direction Skinner went with the wagon. "I want you to keep crawling until you reach the wagon."

Cole unstraps his holster and lets it fall to the ground. He looks at Munroe with resentment.

Munroe is quick to remind him. "We got a deal, Now get on with it."

Cole drops to his knees, then reluctantly places one hand at a time on the ground. When both hands are on the ground Cole starts to crawl in the direction he was told to.

Inside the house...

Tara is watching out the front window still holding Sara. She watches as the Hatchet make Cole crawl. When they are out of sight Tara can't stand it no more. She quickly turns and runs over to the gun rack above the fireplace, she sets Sara down, looks up at the mantle and sees an empty gun rack. A chill runs down her spine as she hears a lever-action rifle being levered behind her and a man's voice.

"Looking for this, honey britches?" asks Ty.

Tara quickly spins around to see Ty holding Cole's rifle. She pulls Sara close to her and Sara wraps her arms tightly around Tara's leg. "What are you doing in my house? Your Colonel said we were free ta go."

Ty starts to walk towards Tara,

Tara pushes Sara behind her.

Ty rubs the rifle barrel gently around Tara's face. "I'm here to make sure you don't interfere with all the fun" "Speaking of which I bet me and you could make our own fun, how bout it, sweet heart?" Ty licks his lips as he runs the rifle barrel down Tara's shoulder toward her breast.

"GO TO HELL, YOU BASTERD!" Tara screams as she grabs the rifle barrel and pushes it away from Sara and herself. She then kicks Ty in the crotch as hard as she can.

Ty lets go of the rifle and falls to his knees holding his groin.

Tara points the rifle at Ty. Tara now knows that they will not let them live. She knows that she will have to fight for her and her daughters lives. Tara knows she has to give Sara time to get away. Tara nudges her daughter with her leg as she holds the rifle on Ty. "RUN, Go to the Terrell's and get help as fast as you can."

Sara is scared, but even as little as she is, she has her parents instinct for survival. "Okay, mama." Sara replies as she bolts for the door as fast as her little legs will carry her.

Just as Sara reaches the front door Ty starts screaming for his partner. "RED! RED GET THE

GIRL SHE'S GOING FOR HELP."

Red steps out of the bedroom and heads for the door.

Tara knows she has to stop him, she raises the rifle and points it at Red and pulls the trigger, but hears a sickening CLICK. She immediately LEVERS the rifle and pulls the trigger again, CLICK. Nothing the rifle is empty.

Red runs out the front door chasing after Sara.

Ty stands back up and smiles. "You didn't think I left it loaded did you?"

Tara desperate to get to her daughter, grabs the rifle by the barrel and tries to hit Ty with the stock of the rifle.

Ty grabs the gun before it can strike him, they both struggle for control of the gun.

Outside...

Sara runs to the shovel she was digging with earlier. She grabs the end of the shovel handle with both hands.

Red screams at her "STOP. You little bitch."

Sara sees Red running toward her. The shovel is big and heavy, but with all of the strength her little body can muster, she spins around and throws the shovel toward Red as hard as she can.

The shovel doesn't go far, but it's far enough. The shovel hits Red in the shins, he trips and tumbles across the ground.

Tara quickly starts to run away once more.

Red yells out in pain and anger. "OW! DAMN IT. YOU LITTLE BITCH, STOP NOW OR I

SWEAR I'LL KILL YA." Red unholsters his revolver and aims at Sara.

Inside the house...

Ty has picked the wrong mother to tangle with. Tara is now sitting straddle on top of Ty chocking him with the rifle as he lays on his back. If she can kill him quickly she can save her daughter.

BANG, A gun shot can be heard from outside.

Tara release her grip and sets up eyes wide, in a state of shock. It's like the life and fight has been sucked out of her body. She knows what has happened. "No. Sara? Not my little Sara." Tara mournfully whispers, as tears run down her face.

Ty reaches under the stock of the rifle and WHACK. He hits Tara upside the head with the rifle stock.

Tara's body slouches and goes limp as she loses consciousness.

"Damn it." Ty mumbles as he pushes Tara off of him and stands up rubbing his neck and coughing. "Your a damn hellcat." He grabs Tara under her arms and drags her to the bedroom.

Just as Ty gets Tara through the bedroom door Red limps in through the front carrying Sara's tiny limp body. Red kicks the front door shut with his foot. He then hears Ty's voice from the bedroom.

"Is that you, Red?"

"Yea, It's me." Red replies.

"What about the little girl?" Ty asks.

"I had to kill her. She almost got away by crippling me." Red answers, as he puts Sara's tiny body on the floor in a corner and walks away from it. "What about the woman?" Red asks as he rubs his shin.

"Damn hellcat almost killed me, she would have too, if she hadn't heard your shot. She's out cold now I'm tying her to the bed."

Ty gets an idea and runs it past Red. "Hey! how about me and you have our turn with her, before the others get back?"

Red doesn't even ponder the idea before answering. "You know the Colonel always goes first. If we went first he'd whip the hide off our backs and we'd be lucky if that's all he done."

Ty responds with disappointment in his voice. "Yea. I know, your right, it was just a thought."

Red shakes his head and adds his own thought. "All that thinking is going to get you killed one of these days. When you ride with the Colonel you don't think, you just follow orders. Make sure she's secure and get out here so your not tempted."

Ty walks out of the bedroom and looks at Sara's body lying on the floor. "So we're baby killers now too, uh?"

Red looks at the body and responds. "Ain't like its the worst thing we ever done. You know we've done a lot worse than this."

Ty gets a look as though he almost feels remorse. "I know, but I think she might be the smallest."

Red gets the same look. "Yea. Me Too." Both men put their feelings aside and walk over to a front window and look out.

There is no room for feelings when you ride with

a group like the Hatchet. Especially when that same group is led by a man like Colonel Munroe Brody. Feelings are like thinking, they both can get you killed.

As Ty and Red stare out the window, Red wonders out loud. "Wonder if they're having fun yet?"

"They should be it's been long enough. I hope they hurry up, I can't stop thinking about that hellcat." Ty says.

Red shakes his head. "There goes that thinking again. Ya know Ty your one smart son of a bitch, its just to bad you do most of your thinking with the wrong head."

Ty simply raises his eyebrows and smiles.

Chapter 5
Beaten But Not Broken

A mile or so from the Hawkins' Ranch...

Cole now with bloodied hands and knees is still crawling as he approaches the wagon.

Skinner is leaning against the wagon enjoying the show.

The rest of the Hatchet are following closely on their horses.

"The punishment fits the crime, Cole. I wanted you to crawl, because my brother was crawling when you killed him. He was crawling away from you and in cold blood you chased him down and slit his throat." Munroe says.

Cole is bloody and tired, but he still won't tolerate lies. "Your brother weren't crawlin' away, he was crawlin' for a gun. He killed two of my

34

friends before I ever reached him." Cole reaches the wagon and stops.

Munroe is furious, he has to justify what he is doing. "DAMN REBEL LIES. ALL OF IT." Munroe yells, then he takes a deep breath and calms himself. "I think you better keep your damn, filthy, rebel mouth shut from here on out. Other wise I might forget about our little deal."

Munroe steps down off of his horse and looks to the men of the Hatchet. "DISMOUNT MEN."

The Hatchet dismount from their horses and gather around Cole.

Munroe motions with his head and says "I want that piece of shit bucked to the wagon."

Clay voices his obedience with a loud "YES SIR, COLONEL."

Clay waves his hand motioning for J.T. to follow him. Both men approach Cole as Skinner gets some rope out of the wagon.

Clay and J.T. pick Cole up to his feet and face him towards the wagon between the wheels, they lay Cole face first over the side of the wagon.

Skinner ties the rope to both of Cole's wrist and spreads his arms tight across the wagon and secures the rope to the other side.

Clay ties one of Cole's legs to a wheel as J.T. ties the other leg to the other wheel.

Munroe reaches into his saddle bag and pulls out a three thong lashing whip, then turns back around to face the men. "Now we're about to have some fun. Who wants the honor?"

Skinner quickly speaks up. "I'd sure enjoy the

hell out of it, Sir."

Munroe smiles proudly. "Then by all means, get to it."

"YES SIR." Skinner enthusiastically replies as he rushes over to Munroe.

Munroe Holding his left arm horizontal in front of himself hands the whip over the top of it with his right hand, as though it were a sacred ritual.

Skinner smiles, nods once and takes the whip. Skinner gets in to position just behind Cole.

Clay rips the back of Cole's shirt open to reveal his bare back.

Skinner looks back to Munroe and asks "You have any particular number in mind, Colonel?"

Munroe looks up as though he is thinking, then looks back at skinner and smiles. "Lets start with Ten."

Skinner nods, spits tobacco juice on the ground rares back and CRACK one lash. You can clearly see whelps form on Cole's back.

Cole grits his teeth and tries to contain his scream as he lets out a muffled "AAAHH!"

Skinner releases the second lash, CRACK.

Cole lets out another muffled scream between gritted teeth.

Each lash leaves more whelps.

CRACK, the third lash finds its mark.

CRACK, the fourth lash.

CRACK, the fifth lash.

CRACK, the sixth lash lands across Cole's back. Cole is still trying to stifle his screams.

CRACK, the seventh lash slams against flesh.

CRACK, the eighth lash draws blood. Cole's screams are now quieter.

CRACK, the ninth lash, more blood.

CRACK, the tenth lash leaves a bloody smear across Cole's back.

Cole is no longer screaming only a faint groan. They say if your body goes through enough trauma, it will numb the area of the trauma. This may be the case with Cole, then again he may have dug deep into his stubborn nature and found his will to resist.

Munroe walks over to Cole and slaps him on the back. "You havin' fun yet Cole? We sure the hell are." Munroe sees the blood on his hand and rubs his fingers together. "Rebel blood feels like honey." Munroe raises his hand up and touches his tongue to the blood, makes a sour face and spits it on the ground. "UGH! God damn it. It may feel like honey, but, it tastes like shit." Munroe wipes the blood off on the back of Skinner's jacket and steps back.

Back at the Hawkins' home...

Red and Ty are looking out the front windows. "How far along do ya think they are, now?" Ty asks.

"I bet they're right in the middle of it by now." Red answers. Red looks around for something to occupy their time and spots food on the table. "Let's eat some of that food on the table, before it spoils."

Ty spots the food and licks his lips. "Yea, I'm starvin'."

Red and Ty walk over to the table and make themselves at home.

At the wagon...

The Hatchet continue to torture Cole. Munroe reaches down and picks up a stick, holding it in both hands, he smashes it across Cole's back. The stick breaks and shatters, pieces flying all around, as Cole winches in pain. Munroe throws the rest of the stick to the ground and smiles at Skinner. "Give em five more."

"Yes, sir." Skinner says. Skinner spits tobacco juice on the ground, rares back, releases and CRACK, lash number one.

Cole barley lets out a low groan. It's still unclear whether Cole has blocked out the pain, passed out or has simply went numb.

Skinner continues, CRACK, lash number two.

CRACK, lash number three, blood runs down Cole's back, yet he gives no response.

CRACK, lash number four.

CRACK, lash number five. Blood splatters the faces of both Skinner and Munroe. Skinner seems to enjoy it, Munroe not so much.

Munroe seems to be getting very agitated. "Why ain't he screaming? This ain't as fun with out him screaming." Munroe walks back up to Cole and knees him in the ass, no response. POP, Munroe punches Cole hard in the side, Cole barely groans.

POP, POP, Munroe punches Cole twice more, still Cole barely responds. "I think he's already through. I thought he was a tough ass Partisan Ranger but, he ain't shit. Cut em loose." Munroe says.

Skinner pulls out his knife and grabs Cole's ear, but before he can cut it off,

Munroe stops him. "Leave his ear in place, I want him to hear me loud and clear."

Skinner is disappointed, but knows not to disobey orders. He cuts the ropes on Cole's feet first, then while holding Cole up he reaches over and cuts the ropes off both of Cole's Wrists. Skinner lets Cole go.

Cole drops limply to the ground on his side then roles to his belly. Cole lays there with no more movement.

WHACK, Munroe kicks Cole, but there is still no response from Cole. Pissed Munroe starts kicking Cole all over the body and legs.

WHACK, WHACK, WHACK, WHACK, He continues for a few more times then turns away and throws his hands up. "You gotta be shittin' me, that's all you got? Your woman could a' took more than that." Still facing away from Cole, Munroe shakes his head in disgust.

Cole's not done yet, he places his hands under his chest and pushes his chest off the ground. Cole brings one knee under himself, then the other.

The men of the hatchet look at each other surprised.

"Uh, Colonel." Skinner says trying to get Munroe's attention.

Munroe turns and sees Cole trying to stand.

Cole now on his hands and knees places his right foot under himself, then puts his right hand on his right knee. Cole shifts his weight backward and kicks his left foot under himself, now in a squatting position with his left hand still on the ground, Cole shifts his butt under himself and places his left hand on his left knee. With a GRUNT he stands, wobbles, then widens his stance to steady himself and looks up at Munroe.

Munroe looks back, with an angry look.

Cole breathing heavily, continues to stand and stares defiantly at Munroe.

The men of the Hatchet look at each other with amazement.

"Damn! He's one tough son of a bitch." J.T. Whispers.

Munroe now pissed stomps back over to Cole. "WHAT? You stood up. Whoop tee do." Munroe says sarcastically. "So what? You think because you stood up your some kind of god damn big man? Well, your not, you still ain't SHIT." Munroe pulls his knife and stabs Cole in the lower abdomen.

Cole buckles over and drops to his hands and knees.

Chapter 6
Sins of the Hatchet

"How about that?" asks Munroe then he continues his rant. "Don't think your going to get off easy though, between the wounds on your back and the one I just gave ya, you'll bleed to death, but it's gonna take awhile."

Munroe starts to turn but, then stops and faces Cole once more. He squats down and lifts Cole's head back, by the hair, to look at him. "By the way I lied, our deals off. Since we can't have no fun with you we're gonna see how much fun we can have with them pretty little ladies of yours. So while your lying here in agony, you think about what we're doing. You make sure you picture every little detail." " I let you keep your ear, maybe if you concentrate real hard you can hear them scream."

With great effort Cole reaches out and grabs Munroe's ankle, then looks him dead in the eye and warns him. "Ya hurt even one hair on their heads, an I swear, Not even hell it's self will keep me from comin' after ya. I'll find ya and I'll kill ya, Whatever it takes I'll do it."

Munroe laughs. "Your gonna come back from hell to kill me, uh? Well then come an get me you god damn, Rebel son of a bitch." Munroe stands back up, pulls his ankle out of Cole's grip and WHACK, kicks Cole in the face. The force of the kick knocks Cole over to his back.

Cole lays motionless on his back blood coming from his mouth and nose.

Munroe turns and heads for his horse. "HATCHET. MOUNT UP AND RIDE." Munroe yells.

All the men of the hatchet, except for Skinner, mount their horses and ride back towards the Hawkins Ranch.

Skinner walks over to Cole and spits Tobacco juice on his head, Then gets in the wagon. "I'll give your regards to the girls." Skinner says taunting Cole. Skinner laughs an evil laugh and adds "I'll give it real good." Skinner slaps the reins hard. "HAW! GET UP! GET GOING YOU SORRY OLD NAGS! HAW! HAW! Skinner turns the wagon and heads back to the ranch right behind the rest of the Hatchet.

Inside the Hawkins' house...
Ty and Red are sitting at the table eating the

supper That Tara had prepared for her family. Red leans back in his chair and rubs his belly. "She's a damn fine cook. Maybe we should keep her around to cook for us."

Ty shakes his head in disagreement. "Hell, she'd poison us the first chance she got."

Red smiles."I suppose your right."

Ty smiles back and says "Hell yea I'm right. Now go see if you can see anything yet."

Red's smile fades from his face. "I went last time, it's your turn."

Ty knows it doesn't take much to set Red off, but the food is good enough to chance it. "Damn it, Red. We ain't taking turns. Your through eatin' and I'm not, so go look."

Red slams his hand on the table. "FINE! Ya damn lazy bastard I'll go look," "*again.*"

Red forcibly slides his chair back, as he stands from the table, then he stomps toward the front window, still bitching. "I guess I'm the only one capable of looking out the damn window." Red looks out the window then leans closer, as though he's trying to see farther in the distance. "HEY! I see em'. Yea, it's them, they're comin' back."

Ty stands quickly from the table and heads towards Red. "It's about damn time." Ty pushes Red to one side and looks out the window. "Hot Damn. We can have some fun now."

Ty and Red both look at each other and smile like two excited kids, then run out the front door.

Back at the torture site...

43

Cole forces himself to sit up. He removes his now ragged shirt and wraps it around his waist and ties it tight to put pressure on the stab wound. As he tightens the shirt he cringes with pain

"AAHH!"

Through labored breathing he mumbles to himself.

"Come on ignore the pain. Focus on your family, you got to help them. Now stand up, Damn it, get going."

Cole rolls over to his hands and knees, with much pain and effort, he puts one foot under him, then does the same with the other. Every move he makes is exhausting and sends pain coursing through his body. This won't stop him, he's light headed, but he's more determined than anything else.

Cole's biggest flaw is his mule headed stubbornness, but in times like this, it becomes his biggest asset. Once he sets his mind to do something he'll either do it, or die trying.

Cole now in a squatting position, grits his teeth, groans, stands up, wobbles, stumbles and then catches his balance. Breathing heavy and holding his stab wound he takes a step.

Then a second step.

A third step.

A forth, then stumbles and falls to his hands and knees. Cole is now almost delirious from the pain, but he pushes through.

"Don't stop, you can't give up, they need you. Get up, Damn you get up"

With raw determination Cole once more struggles to stand. Once more, with one foot at a time and with great effort and pain, he's back on his feet. He slowly staggers towards his destination.

A couple of hours later...

Back at the Hawkins' Ranch, the Hatchet are loitering about. Munroe and Wade are leaning against the front porch railing, talking to each other.

Jack and Jake are in front practicing with their sabers.

J.T., Buck, Clay, Emmett, TY and Red are out at the corral watching the horses.

Preacher is leaning against the wagon reading his bible.

Tenderfoot is standing behind preacher pestering him, by touching Preachers ear with a long weed every now and then. When preacher looks at Tenderfoot, Tenderfoot hides the weed by crossing his arms and then leans his back against the wagon.

The Hatchet's horses are tied to the fences close to the wagon.

Skinner comes out the front door buttoning his trousers.

Munroe turns to see skinner. "You get done?" Munroe asks.

"Yes sir." Skinner answers, then he gets a curious look and asks "Um, Colonel, how come I'm always the last to get a turn?"

Munroe looks him up and down then responds. "Cause your filthy and disgusting and you stink to high heaven."

45

Skinner looks kind of confused. "That's the only reason?"

"Pretty much. If you would take a bath more than twice a year, you might get to take an earlier turn. You should start taking a bath every couple of months like the rest of us." Munroe says.

Skinner looks as though he is shocked. "Every couple a months?"

"I got sensitive skin, Colonel. Taking a bath that often would wash the skin right off my bones." Skinner steps off the porch, shaking his head and mumbling to himself, what he says is not understandable, just mumbled gibberish.

"Hey!" Munroe says to get Skinner's attention.

Skinner turns and timidly looks back up at Munroe, hoping he's not in trouble. "Yes, Colonel."

Munroe knows that Skinner is scared, he enjoys men fearing him, so he lingers it out a bit, before asking "The woman still alive?"

Skinner lets out a breath, relieved he's not in trouble. "No, sir. She was dead before I ever got my turn."

All the men of the Hatchet start to walk towards Munroe.

"Did ya skin her?" Munroe asks.

"No, sir. She was so beat up after everyone had their way with her, I didn't see the point" "I did skin the little one though." Skinner reaches down to the leather thong fastened around his belt, grabs and holds up a tiny ear.

At this time all the men of the Hatchet are now standing close enough to hear and see what's going on.

Each of the men cringe or make a unique face when skinner holds up the ear. These are evil heartless men, but this is to much even for them.

Munroe shakes his head in disgust. "Your one sick bastard, Skinner."

Skinner smiles proudly as though it was a compliment. "Thank you, sir."

Wade steps forward and asks "Orders sir?"

Munroe looks at the Hatchet and responds. "I want the bodies put on display right out front here. Then burn every structure to the ground, tear down the corrals secure what horses you can and scatter the rest."

Wade nods, "Yes, sir. Consider it done." Wade turns around and addresses the Hatchet. "YOU HEARD THE COLONEL. GET IT DONE."

Skinner and Emmett head inside the house, the rest of the men scatter to do other chores.

Hours later...

Cole now covered in mud and blood, slowly drags his feet with each step. He has blacked out many times on this long journey, but he will not quit. He doesn't know how much time has passed, but he is going as fast as he possibly can.

As he reaches the ranch, he can hardly hold his head up, but he manages to raise his head enough to see the smoldering remains of his property. He stumbles and falls. Lying on his stomach he strains to push himself off the ground, but fails. Once more he pushes as hard as he can, but he no longer has the strength and collapses to the ground.

He doesn't have the strength, but he does have the determination, breathing heavily, he grits his teeth and starts to crawl, dragging his body towards his goal. When he gets close to what use to be the front of his house, he struggles once more and manages to look up. What he sees is what no one should ever have to see.

Two posts have been driven into the ground strapped to the post are the bodies of Cole's wife Tara and his tiny Daughter Sara. Cole reaches out for them with tears running down his face, streaking the mud and blood that covers it. He reaches hard, his eyes roll back in his head and he collapses. It's like the life as been drained out of his body.

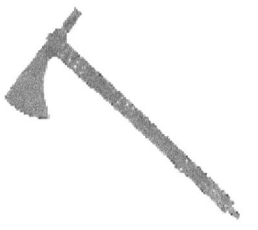

Chapter 7
Help on the Horizon

In the distance...

Approaching Hawkins Ranch is a man and women in an old buck board wagon, being pulled by two mares. A boy on a horse rides along the side of the wagon.

The man is Frank Terrell, he is in his late fifties with an average build, he has one crippled leg and one crippled arm.

The woman is Mary Terrell, Frank's wife she is in her late forties and in very good shape.

The boy is Ethan Terrell, a slender young man in his early to mid teens, he is Frank and Mary Terrell's only son.

As the Terrell's get closer to the Hawkins Ranch Mary spots the smoke. "Frank somethings burning, do you see it?"

Frank looks in the direction of the smoke, but doesn't seem concerned. "Yea I see it, Mary. Might be a brush fire or somethin'."

Mary is a little more observant and does not believe this to be a simple brush fire, there's to much black smoke. Mary strains to see what it is. "I don't think so. That looks like it's at the..."

Almost instantly it hits her and she realizes what it is. "OH MY GAWD. FRANK THATS THE HAWKINS' PLACE." she yells.

Mary and Frank both look at each other with worried looks.

Frank turns his head to face forwards again and slaps the reins hard. "HEYAA! HEYAA!" He yells at the mares. The wagon jerks forward with great force as the mares bolt and pick up speed. Frank turns and yells to his son. "COME ON ETHAN THE HAWKINS' PLACE IS ON FIRE."

Ethan without saying a word kicks his horse with his heels and bolts after his folks.

When they get close enough they can see that they're to late, the only thing left is smoldering ruins. Then they spot the bodies.

Mary opens her mouth and quickly places her hands over it in shock, then slowly lowers her hands. "Oh my Gawd. Who would do such a thing?"

Frank shakes his head in disbelief "Some kind a' savages." "We can't leave them like this, lets give em' a proper burial, then we'll notify the Sheriff."

Frank and Mary climb down from the wagon,

Mary grabs some blankets out of the back of the wagon before stepping down.

Ethan dismounts from his horse and they all approach the bodies.

"Wait." Mary says.

Frank and Ethan both stop and face Mary to hear whats on her mind.

"You two take care of Cole. I'll take care of Tara and little Sara." "It wouldn't be proper for you men to touch em' before I get their bodies covered."

Frank nods in agreement. "Your right Mary. Can you do it by yourself?"

"I'll manage." Answers Mary.

Frank knows she will. "You always do."

He knows she is strong in body and will, if something needs doing, when Mary's around, it'll get done.

Frank turns and speaks to his son. "Ethan, Come and help me son."

Ethan nods and responds with a simple, "Yes Pa."

A short time later...

Tara's body is on the ground wrapped in a blanket. Mary lays Sara's tiny body on another blanket and wraps it up. Mary's a strong woman, but she can't take it in any longer and starts to sob. "She's just a baby. Why? WHY?"

Frank walks as fast as he can back to Mary, sits next to her and holds her in his arms.

"Her skins gone." Mary says. "How could someone do that to a baby?"

Frank doesn't know how to answer her, he can barely contain his own emotions. "I, I don't know, I don't know how anyone could be capable of any of this. Cole looks like he's been tortured to death."

Ethan is squatting down next to Cole wiping the blood and mud from his face with a rag, at least he's trying to, the best he can.

Cole takes a labored breath and groans.

Ethan surprised, stands up and takes a step backward. "MA, PA, HE'S ALIVE. COLES ALIVE."

Mary stands and helps Frank to his feet, they both hurry over to Cole. Mary reaches him first kneels down next to him and gently places one of her hands on Cole's Chest and leans her ear close to his face. It's one of the best sounds she has heard in a long time. It's faint, but Cole's breathing. "Your right. He is alive."

Mary knows they have to act quickly. She also knows that with Frank's bad arm and leg it takes him the longest to get in the wagon, so he's the first one she addresses. "Frank, get in the wagon."

Frank doesn't hesitate, he starts for the wagon.

Mary then turns her attention to her son. "Ethan, help me get Cole in the back of the wagon."

Ethan doesn't say anything he just acts. Mary and Ethan put Cole in the back of the wagon, while Frank climbs into the seat.

Mary grabs her son by the shoulders and turns him to face her. "I want you to go get Doc Preston and send him to our place. Once you've done that come back here and dig graves for the girls and you make sure your respectful."

Ethan nods "I will be Ma."

Mary pulls Ethan close and gives him a hug. "Once I get Cole settled, I'll come back here and help you."

Mary lets Ethan go and gently pushes him away. "Now get going. Hurry as fast as you can, but be careful."

Ethan nods once more. "I will Ma."

Ethan gets on his horse and bolts out in a dead run.

Mary quickly climbs into the wagon next to Frank.

Frank slaps the reins. "Hold on tight." He tells Mary, then yells to the mares. "HEYAA! HEYAA! GET UP GIRLS."

The wagon bolts forward and the Terrell's rush for home. Cole would not have survived a wagon trip to town. The closest place is the Terrell's homestead. They will have to bring the doctor to Cole and hope for the best.

A couple of hours later...

at the Terrell homestead, Frank Terrell is pacing outside a bedroom door. Doctor Mitchell Preston, an elderly and experienced Doctor with gray hair and a slender build, walks out of the bedroom, wearing glasses and carrying a black Doctors bag.

Frank stops pacing and turns to face the Doc. "How is he Doc?"

Doc Preston rubs the back of his neck as though it was sore from looking down for a long time.

"Hard to say." "I've done all I can for him, the rest is up to him."

Frank nods slightly. "Is there anything we can do?"

Doc Preston shakes his head. "Not really. Just try to keep him comfortable, you already did all you could."

Doc Preston removes his glasses and places them in his front pocket. "Bringing him to your house gave him a chance, if you would have tried to bring him all the way to town, he wouldn't have survived the trip."

Frank nods in agreement. "That was Mary's doing, she use ta be a nurse before we came out west."

Doc Preston walks over to the door and puts his hand on the handle. "She definitely gave him a fighting chance." "If you don't mind me asking? Where is Mrs. Terrell?"

Frank's eyes go sad. "Her and my boy Ethan are burying Cole's wife and daughter."

Doc Preston gets a surprised look on his face. "The men who done this to him, also killed his wife and daughter?" He asks.

Frank nods affirmatively. "Yes sir."

Doc Preston shakes his head in sympathy. "I'm sorry to hear that."

Tears form in Doc Preston's eyes. "I brought little Sara into this world." "Brought her through the smallpox too."

Doc Preston wipes the tears from his face and tries to compose himself. "It seems that there is more and more cruelty happening every day."

Frank nods again. "It sure does Doc."

Frank steers the conversation back to Cole. "So as for Cole, we just wait and see?"

Doc Preston is relieved to talk about something else. "That's it. He's been whipped, beat, stabbed and who knows what else." "He's lucky to have lasted this long."

Doc Preston smiles just a little. "But he's a fighter so if he makes it through the night, I'd give him a pretty good chance of surviving this."

Doc Preston turns toward the door then looks back. "If he does pull through have Mrs. Terrell change his bandages regularly and" "well she knows what shes doing. I got other rounds to make so I best be going. Give Mrs. Terrell and Ethan my best"

Doc Preston opens the front door.

"I will Doc." Frank says. "What do I owe you for today?" "I would just as soon square up with you now if I can."

Doc Preston smiles and shakes his head. "Since there wasn't much I could do for him, it's on the house."

Frank smiles. "Thanks Doc."

Doc Preston winks and says, "That's okay, I'll just charge you double next time."

With that statement he walks out the door, he has many more rounds to make before his night is through. Frank smiles and shuts the door behind him, then walks back to the bedroom to check on Cole.

Chapter 8
Gathering Strength and Tools

Several weeks later...
outside the Terrell's home. The Terrell's
homestead is a small farm, it has a home, a small
barn, a chicken coop, a pig pen and a small garden.

Near one side of the house Cole, shirtless with
bandages still wrapped around his waist for his ribs
and stab wound, is chopping fire wood with an ax.
Cole's back is covered with scars from the lashings.
There is a large log, which he places the smaller
ones on. With one stroke, Cole splits the logs like it
is easy and natural.

Frank approaches him from behind. "Ya look
like your feeling better, but ya probably shouldn't be
doing that." "As a matter of fact if Mary sees ya,
shes gonna tan both our hides."

Cole turns to face Frank. "After everything y'all have done for me, the least I can do is help out with some of the chores. If there's anything ya need me ta do, ya just holler and I'll get to it."

Then they hear Mary's angry voice. "COLE HAWKINS."

Cole and Frank look to see Mary Stomping towards them.

"Uh oh, we've had it now." Frank whispers.

Mary is more concerned than angry, but it still comes across as anger. "What in tarnation do you think your doing out here chopping wood, still bandaged like you are?" It's more a statement than a question and she gives them no time to answer. "Its a wonder you ain't popped those stitches wide open."

Mary puts her hands on her hips and gives Cole *the look*, the one only a women can give that lets every man know they mean business. Then she shakes her finger at Frank. "And you Frank Terrell, standing right there and watching him do it."

Mary puts both hands back on her hips and gives Frank an extra potent *look*.

Cole tries to defend Frank. "It weren't his fault..."

Frank interrupts, before Cole has a chance of digging himself any deeper. "Never mind, when she's like this it's best just ta shut up and take the chewin', and hope ya got some backside left when she's done."

Mary tries to fight back a smile, but she just can't

stay mad, she shakes her head back and forth. "I don't know what I'm gonna do with you Two."

Cole gets his chance to explain. "I appreciate all you've done for me, ma'am, but I'm feelin' awful cooped up lying in that bed all day."

Mary nods in agreement. "Well, I suppose a little work will help you get yer strength back and keep you from stiffenin' up."

Mary then points her finger at Cole and gives him another *look*. "You just don't go over doing it. Ya hear me?"

Cole smiles and nods. "Yes ma'am."

Mary smiles back. "Now that we've settled that, breakfast is ready. You boys get Ethan and come an eat, then you can get back to yer chores."

Mary turns and heads back to the house.

Frank looks in the direction of the barn and yells for Ethan. "ETHAN, COME AND EAT BREAKFAST SON.

Ethan yells back from inside the barn. "I'LL BE RIGHT THERE PA."

Cole and Frank nod at each and head inside to get some breakfast.

Miles away...

The Hatchet's hideout is an old two story farm house with a big barn and a few smaller out buildings. The Hatchet has placed logs vertically all the way around these buildings, to make it look more like a fort. There is one opening for the exit and entrance, the gates are open and never shut. The Hatchet believe no one would ever be brave enough to attack them here.

Munroe and Wade walk out onto the porch. Munroe is stretching and Wade is yawning and stretching, they both have just awakened. "What do you have planned for today, Colonel?" Wade asks.

"I want you and Clay to take one of the wagons and meet up with our Mexican friends out at slippery rock pass." Munroe responds. "They got us some crates of dynamite. Me and the rest of the boys are going to see if we can stir up more trouble."

Wade smiles. "What about the Bean Eaters, you want us to pay em, or kill em'?"

Munroe slightly shrugs. "I'm gonna leave that up to your discretion. Just be careful with the dynamite, take your time and get it back here in one peace."

"Yes Sir! We'll leave right after breakfast." Wade says.

"We all will. We'll meet back here in a few days." Munroe adds.

Wade nods in agreement and both men walk back into the house.

Back at the Terrell Homestead...

It is now night, Cole, Frank, Mary and Ethan are sitting on the front porch. Frank and Mary are on one side in rockers, Mary is mending a pair of pants and frank is smoking a pipe. There is a coal oil lamp on a small stand next to Mary. Cole is on the other side of the porch, leaning back in a rocker with his feet on the porch railing and his hands behind his head, he is staring out at the night sky. Ethan is sitting on the porch steps working on something, but trying not to draw attention to it.

"I reckon I best be headin' out in the morning." Cole says.

Mary looks concerned as though Cole's statement took her off guard. "So soon? I'm not sure your healed enough yet."

Frank knows she's just trying to stall. "Now Mary you know he's heeled just fine."

Mary slightly ducks her head. "I know. I just hate to see him leave."

Mary directs her conversation to Cole. "I know your going after those Hatchet men and after what they done, I'm not gonna try to talk you out of it." "Just promise me you'll be careful and you'll come back to see us again."

Cole puts both feet on the porch and sets up in his rocker. "Yes ma'am I'll do my best."

Frank chimes in. "From what I hear the Hatchet is made up of thirteen of the most vilest and meanest men ya could ever meet."

Cole looks surprised. "Thirteen? I only saw eleven."

Frank gives Cole a sympathetic look. They both know where the other two Hatchet men were, but it won't be spoken of.

"There's thirteen" Frank continues "and everyone of em's pure evil through and through. You more than likely won't get any help from the law. Most of the law is skeared of em' the ones that ain't agree with what they're doing. So yore gonna be going up against em' alone."

Frank holds up his crippled hand. "If I were able, I'd be right there beside ya."

Cole nods. "I never doubted it. Y'all have done more n' enough for me, I don't expect no more." "I won't ever be able to repay ya, as it is."

Frank smiles. "You would a' done the same."

Cole nods once in agreement.

Ethan quickly stands and faces everyone. "I can go with him. I'll fight the Hatchet right beside him."

No one responds and everyone avoids making eye contact with Ethan. Ethan pleads to Cole. "Mr. Hawkins I can ride and shoot, I ain't claimin' to be the best, but I know I can help you and I won't let you down."

Ethan then pleads to his parents. "I'm old enough now Pa." "Ma?"

Cole stands up and looks Ethan in the Eyes. "There's no doubt in my mind ya can scrap with the best of em' and I would be honored to fight beside a man such as yore self."

Ethan's eyes get wide with excitement and Cole continues. "However we don't know were the Hatchet are and they could come back this way. If they do ya need to be here to protect your folks."

Ethan is now starting to realize how important it is to be here. Cole puts his hand on Ethan's shoulder to let him know the question he is going to ask is important. "Can ya look after yore Ma and Pa while I'm gone?"

Ethan stands up straight and tall ready for the challenge. "Yes Sir. I won't let nuthin' happen to em'."

Cole smiles and slaps Ethan on the arm. "Yore a good man, I knew I could count on ya, and I'm proud ta know ya."

Ethan now with a proud smile on his face sits back down on the steps and stares out at the night, like he's daydreaming of a glorious battle.

Cole sits back down in his rocker and looks at Frank and Mary. Mary smiles and to prevent Ethan from knowing, Thanks Cole with a simple nod and smile. Cole understands and nods his head and smiles back.

After a brief moment Frank calls to his son. "Ethan."

Ethan turns to look at Frank. "Yea Pa?"

"Go in the house and get the new Remingtons and my Winchester." Frank says.

Ethan stands and nods. "Yes sir" He heads for the door, but before he can enter. "OH! Ethan bring the holster back too." Frank adds. "Okay Pa." Ethan enters the house.

Inside...

 Ethan walks through the front door, walks over to the mantle and grabs a Winchester rifle and a holster. He lays them by the front door, then heads to the back bedroom and enters.

Outside...

Frank leans forward in his rocker and smiles at Cole. "I can't go with ya and I can't send my boy with ya, but I can make sure you got the proper tools for the job."

"What are ya talkin' about, Frank?" Cole asks.
Frank answers with a simple, "You'll see."

Cole sits back and ponders what Frank is up to.

Everyone can hear Ethan quickly hurrying back, then he opens the door and comes out on the porch holding items wrapped in soft buckskin. He lays the items in Frank's lap and stands close by. Frank unwraps the items and grabs the first, a lever-action Winchester model 1873 rifle. Frank holds up the rifle and hands it to Ethan. "Take that to Cole"

Ethan hands the rifle to Cole and frank states, "That's my Winchester you might find that useful"

Cole looks it over and works the action, he continues to admire the rifle as Ethan walks back to Frank. "Yore really gonna like these" Frank says, as he holds up Two revolvers. One is a *Remington 1875 Frontier*. The other is a *Remington 1875 Army Outlaw*. These two guns are identical except the frontier has a five and a half inch barrel and the outlaw has a seven and a half inch barrel. Frank puts the Army Outlaw in a holster and hands them both to Ethan. "Give em those too."

Ethan walks over and hands Cole the revolvers as frank says, "Those are Remington's new models."

Cole leans the rifle against the porch railing and then takes the holster and revolvers from Ethan. Ethan leans against the porch railing to watch Cole. Cole holds the Frontier in his hand and spins the cylinder to make sure it's empty. He looks at it with great admiration, he spins it backward, then

63

forwards and lays it on a stand next to him. He pulls the Army Outlaw out of the holster and again rotates the cylinder to check it. He admires the workmanship, then spins it backwards then forwards and replaces it in the holster. It's very easy to see that Cole is familiar with handling revolvers.

Cole looks at Frank. "Those are some mighty fine weapons, mighty fine indeed." "Ya need to keep them here."

Frank shakes his head in disagreement. "Yore gonna need em' more than me. Besides me not be able to help ya directly," "well, it'll make me feel a little better if ya take em'."

Cole is very appreciative. "I don't know what ta say." "I'll try and get em' back to ya in the same condition."

Frank shakes his head again. "No, Ya don't understand." "What ya have to do is a personal thing and the tools a man uses to do such a deed should be his own. Those are yore's ta keep."

"Its too much. Y'all have already done more than I can ever repay already." Cole says.

Frank leans forward, with a look that says he needs to do this. "It would give me great honor and pride if ya would except them"

Cole understands a man's pride all to well. "Okay. Thank ya, Thank all of ya."

Cole looks at each of the Terrell's with great appreciation, not knowing how he will ever repay them.

Ethan goes down the steps and grabs what he was working on, he hides it behind his back and returns to Cole. " I have something for you too, Mr. Hawkins. It's not much." "I just found your knife at your place, it was charred and dirty, so I cleaned it up and put a new handle on it."

Ethan brings the knife out from around his back and hands it to Cole.The knife is a custom made civil war era rifleman's fighting knife. It is polished with a brand new handle and lanyard, it is a magnificent work of art. This knife has saved Cole's life more times than he cares to count. He thought it was gone for good.

Cole looks at the knife in a state of awe. He holds the knife in a reverse grip in his left hand. Then he puts his left thumb through the lanyard and lets go with his left hand. With the knife hanging from his right thumb Cole swings the knife around to a saber grip in a fluid motion, then just as smoothly he swings it around to a reverse grip. Ethan looks on in amazement at how Cole can manipulate a blade.

Cole, once again admires the workmanship of the handle, then he looks up at Ethan and smiles. "Feels good." "Feels right." "I thought I had lost this, it means a great deal to me. Thank ya Ethan."

Cole now feels even more beholding to the Terrells. "Thank all of ya. I appreciate everything y'all have done for me." "I hope someday I can find away to repay ya."

Frank stands up and looks at Cole. "Ya can repay us." "Ya can repay us by sending those monsters to hell. Men like that shouldn't be able to roam around killin' without someone trying to stop em'."

Frank points to Cole. "Yore the only one willing and able to go up against em'. Ya put that murderin' scum where they belong and that will be payment enough for us and anyone else who has ever met the Hatchet."

Cole looks at Frank and nods his head. He knows it is not just simple revenge he is after. The Hatchet leave a trail of blood and tears wherever they go. They must be stopped at all cost. Cole is not sure whether he feels revenge or justice is more important. Maybe they both carry the same weight, if it even matters. What he does know is that he has a hard trail ahead. He will have to embrace the violence he was once ashamed of in order to bury the Hatchet.

Chapter 9
Wolves In Army Clothing

The next morning at the charred remains of the Hawkins Ranch, Cole is kneeling between two graves, his hat is laying on the ground in front of him. Cole's horse is standing near by. One Grave is normal sized and the other is small or child sized. The appearance of the graves suggest that someone placed them with great care and effort.

There is a wooden grave marker at the head of each grave. The first reads, "*TARA HAWKINS*" in large letters, below this in smaller letters it reads, "*Loving mother, wife and neighbor. Endowed with a rare kindness that few others possess.*"

The second marker for the small grave reads, "*SARA HAWKINS*", in large letters and under this in smaller letters it reads, "*A precious baby girl who was loved by all. We will look to the heavens with envy knowing that God could not have chosen a more perfect little angel.*"

Cole with head down kisses one hand and places it on Sara's grave, then kisses the other hand and places it on Tara's grave. "I love ya both, I love ya more than I could ever express. I'll love ya always and forever. Ya were everything ta me, and all I ever wanted or needed."

Cole looks up as tears run down his cheeks, He grabs his hat, stands to his feet and puts his hat on his head. He has the gun belt on with the *Outlaw* in the holster in the strong side draw position for his right hand. His knife is fastened to a belt underneath the gun belt on his left side, in a cross draw position. The *Frontier* is tucked in his waist band in the small of his back, turned so he can grab it with his left hand.

Cole looks at the graves of his wife and child. "Now I have nothing, and I swear ta gawd the men who took ya from me will pay, Even if it's the last thing I ever do"

Cole walks over and mounts his horse, he then looks back at the graves. "They took ya from me, now I'm gonna take from them. While y'all rest in heaven, I'm gonna send the Hatchet ta hell."

Cole gently kicks his horse and rides away.

Several miles away...

Eleven of the Hatchet are on a hill overlooking the Jackson homestead, Wade and Clay are not present. Skinner is in the wagon as before and the other ten are mounted on horses.

The Smith homestead is a very small, freshly started spread, consisting of a log cabin and a partially built shed. It is being attacked by Indians. There are two rifles being fired from the cabin.

"Orders Colonel?" Jack asks.

"Open the ball Sergeant and give no quarter." Munroe replies.

Jack turns to address the Hatchet. "Lets get to it men. CHARGE!"

The hatchet charge down the hill, guns blazing. Almost every shot the Hatchet fires hits its mark, felling one Indian after another.

Inside the cabin...

Isiah Jackson, a large, burly, black man in his forties, is firing out one window of the cabin with a rifle. The rifle runs out of ammo, Isiah hands the rifle back to his father. "Rifles empty Pa."

Noah Jackson, Isiah's father, a frail, elderly, black man with gray hair and beard takes the rifle and hands Isiah a revolver. Noah begins reloading the rifle, as Isiah fires out the window with the revolver. After firing three shots Isiah looks over to his wife, at the other window. "How ya doin' Emma?"

Emma Jackson, Isiah's wife, a strong willed, slightly over weight, black woman in her late thirties or early forties fires one barrel of a double barreled shotgun out another window. BLAM. The kick from the shotgun jars her backward, she steps back into it and fires the other barrel. BLAM. She hands the empty shotgun to Abigail Jackson, Isiah and Emma's daughter, a small preteen black girl. Abigail hands Emma a revolver. Emma takes the revolver and then replies to her husband. "I'm fine Isiah. Stop frettin' over me. Do more shootin' and less jawin'."

Emma looks at Abigail and smiles. "Yore doin' fine Abigail. Just concentrate on loading and don't even think about whats happenin' outside."

Frightened Abigail nods " Yes mama."

Emma turns back around and fires the pistol out the window. Abigail folds the shotgun open, removes the spent shotgun shells, places two fresh shells into the holes, snaps the shotgun shut and readies it for when her mama needs it. She may be small, but she's already becoming an old pro at loading the guns.

Isiah stops firing and looks closer out the window. "STOP. STOP SHOOTIN'." He yells.

Emma stops firing and everyone looks at Isiah. "Its the Calvary. The Calvary is outside fightin' the Indians."

Everyone, excitedly rushes to a window to look outside. Emma lets out a sigh and expresses her relief. "Oh thank heavens. I thought we were done fer."

Emma then expresses her concerns for her family. "Is everyone okay? Abigail?"

"I'm okay mama." Answers Abigail.

Emma continues. "Isiah? Papa Noah? You men didn't take a bullet did'ja?"

Noah looks himself over. "I'm still breathin'."

Isiah smiles and nods. "I'm fine too Em. I'm gonna go meet the Calvary. Y'all stay here till we know its safe."

Isiah hands his revolver to Noah. "Don't ya think ya might need that son?" Noah asks.

Isiah shakes his head. "No Pa. They just saved our lives, I don't wanna appear ungrateful or aggressive."

Isiah walks to the front door and walks outside.

Outside the cabin...

Isiah walks over to Munroe who is standing in front of the cabin holding the reins of his horse. Jack, Jake and J.T. are standing near by slightly behind Munroe. Skinner is taking scalps from the dead Indians and the rest of the Hatchet are still mounted in the near distance.

Isiah smiles and addresses Munroe "Am I glad to see y'all. Mister I done thought we were goners and low and behold we're saved by the Calvary."

Munroe doesn't seem to friendly. Isiah sees Skinner scalping the dead bodies of the Indians. "I don't mean ta seem ungrateful but, is that really necessary?" He asks.

"They did try to kill us, but I was raised to respect the dead."

Now fairly agitated, Munroe shows his arrogance. "First, them savages don't deserve no respect. Second, Scalps are worth money. Third I'm not a Mr. and we're not a Calvary."

Isiah is confused by Munroe's demeanor. "Excuse me?"

Munroe rolls his eyes as though he thinks he's talking to an idiot. "I'm a Colonel, Colonel Munroe Brody and we are a Dragoon not a Calvary."

Isiah continues to be friendly. "I'm sorry I meant no disrespect, Colonel." "I ain't a military man so I don't know the difference."

Munroe steps a little closer to Isiah. Jack and Jake hand their reins to J.T. and start to slowly move around to position themselves behind Isiah. Munroe becomes even more arrogant and slightly slows his speech. "Let me explain it to you then for future reference. Mounted soldiers use horses for transportation but, they are trained to fight from the ground. A Calvary is trained to fight from horseback. A Dragoon, me and my men are trained to fight from both, any time, anyplace, from any position and by any means."

Isiah is noticeably offended by Munroe's sarcastic attitude, but he tries to ignore it and remain hospitable. "I see, next time I'll know the difference. Anyway, you and your men saved our lives and I am mighty grateful..."

"That would make twice now." Munroe interrupts.

Isiah is confused by the comment. "Twice?" "I don't understand?"

Munroe rolls his eyes yet again. "We saved you today and during the war, when we freed you from slavery."

Isiah is a patient man, but he is to proud to tolerate this. He has to set the record straight so to speak. "No disrespect Colonel but, I was a free man before the war. We worked for a Confederate General who wanted to make sure no one thought he was fighting for slavery, he fought for state rights and the way of the south."

Munroe is becoming noticeably angry as Isiah continues. "He treated us with respect and payed us a fair wage. He was killed by Yankees and Yankees burned down the plantation including my families place."

Munroe is down right furious now, but Isiah is going to say his piece. "They left us homeless that's why we came out west. My mama didn't survive the trip. So again, Colonel no disrespect intended but I am a free man because of a great and honorable southern gentlemen not because of some Yankee war."

Munroe is now beyond furious, he is so mad he is shaking. "Men died in a war for you ungrateful heathen bastards and now my men risk their lives again and" "You ain't nothing but a damn shaded puke."

Munroe looks at Jack and Jake, who are now positioned behind Isiah. "Stick this black son of a bitch like a pig."

Jack and Jake both draw their sabers. Isiah tries to turn and defend himself but, its to late. Jack sticks his saber through Isiah's side it goes in one side and comes out the other at the back. Jake sticks his saber clean through Isiah's neck. Isiah drops to his knees, then falls forward, dead. Jack kicks him just to make sure and then taunts. "Oink, oink. Say goodnight little dark piggy."

Skinner comes running over to Munroe, skinner is carrying a tomahawk when he approaches. "COLONEL."

Munroe turns to face Skinner, who hands Munroe the tomahawk. "Thought you might want this for a keepsake Colonel" Skinner says.

Munroe takes the tomahawk and checks its weight and balance, he flips it into the air for a half rotation and catches it by the handle. The Hatchet are acting as though nothing has happened, death means nothing to them.

Munroe continues to admire the tomahawk. "That's a mighty fine war weapon, mighty fine indeed. You did good Skinner, Thanks."

"Anytime Sir." Skinner says as he turns and proudly walks away to finish scalping.

Inside the cabin...

Emma sees what happened to her husband, she steps away from the window and grabs her mouth before she can scream.

"What is it Mama?" Abigail asks.

Emma grabs Abigail and hugs her. "Nothing, Nothing that you need to worry about, just yet."

Noah, who also saw what happened, grabs Emma and Abigail and pushes them toward the back door. "Y'all need ta git. Go out the back door an git to the house down by the crick, the people who live there will help ya."

Emma resists. "What about you Papa Noah?" "You have to come with us."

Noah shakes his head. "I wouldn't make it, I'm to

old and slow, but I can slow these damn yanks down long enough for you. It's all an old man has left and if I can go out protecting my family, then I can go out proud. NOW GIT."

Emma doesn't like it one bit, but she knows that her daughters safety must come first. She grabs her shotgun and pulls Abigail out the back door as Noah grabs the rifle and heads for the front door. Noah waits and listens by the front door. He's going to give Emma and Abigail as much distance as he can.

Outside...

The men of the Hatchet are still relatively in the same positions. Jack has one foot on Isiah's body and is looking toward Munroe, who is still flipping and catching the tomahawk. Munroe grabs the blade end of the tomahawk and slides the handle under his gun belt on his left side. He pats the tomahawk, then looks up at Jack. "There was more than one shooter in that cabin, when we rode up. You an Jake search the house to see how many more pukes are inside."

Jack slaps Jake on the arm and motions with his head to 'come on.' Jake starts to follow Jack to the front porch. The front door quickly swings inward and Noah with rifle in-hand steps out. "I'm the only one left and I'd rather be a puke than a damn yeller bellied Yankee. So you sum bitch's can stick a feather in yore hat and go ta hell."

Noah raises the rifle to his shoulder, as Jack rushes toward him and pushes the barrel away just as the rifle fires. Jack then punches Noah with the other hand, Noah lets go of the rifle and falls back against the cabin then to the ground. Jake draws his saber pulls it back ready to stab Isiah. "HOLD IT." Munroe yells.

Jake relaxes and looks toward Munroe.

"We got ourselves a proud black man here who wants to go out in a blaze of glory. I say we give him his wish." Munroe says.

"Bring him out into the middle of the yard" he says as he motions with his hand.

"Yes Sir." Jake says as he sheathes his saber.

Jake grabs Noah and yanks him up to his feet and drags him off the porch and into the open. Jake pushes Noah away from himself and backs away. Noah stumbles, but manages to stay on his feet.

"HATCHET FORM A LINE" Munroe yells as he motions with his hand.

The Hatchet come forward and form a line in front of Isiah. Munroe Raises his hand high over his head. "Prepare to fire."

The men of the Hatchet raise their weapons, some have rifles others have revolvers, they all point them at Noah.

Noah shows no fear. "That's right you gosh dern, lily livered, yeller bellied, Yankee doodling, sissy britches, prepare to farr on an unarmed, old codger."

Munroe smiles dominantly at Noah. Noah looks Munroe straight in the eyes, stands up straight and proud and smiles right back at Munroe. "Go on an git er done ya murderin' Yankee bastard." Isiah taunts.

Munroe's smile turns to an angry scowl and he rapidly pulls his hand down. "FIRE."

A volley of shots ring out as the Hatchet open fire. Noah is struck by dozens of bullets, his head drops but, his pride won't let his body fall, not yet. Noah raises his head up and looks defiantly at Munroe, then pans his head to the rest of the hatchet and back to Munroe. The men of the Hatchet, in a state of shock, look at each other then stare back at Noah. Noah continues to defiantly and proudly taunt the Hatchet. "That all ya yanks can muster? Ya may as' well go on home an put some skirts on, cause ya ain't nuthin', but a bunch of sissy girly men."

Noah staggering but, fighting to stay on his feet spits toward Munroe, smiles once more then drops to his knees. Still struggling to remain upright, Noah drops to his hands, he's trying so hard to remain upright that he's shaking, then finally he collapses to the ground. Munroe walks away embarrassed, an old man just showed him up.

Chapter 10
The Hatchet Prey Again

Later after the Hatchet have left...

The Jackson's property is now nothing but charred remains, Emma and Abigail stand next to two fresh graves marked by simple stick crosses. Tears run down Abigail's face. Emma hides her emotions, she has to be strong for Abigail. There is also a wagon close by with an elderly couple sitting in the wagon seat.

The couple are Sam Taggert, a heavy set old man and his wife, Ruth Taggert, a frail looking old woman. Mr. Taggert is holding the reins.

Emma and Abigail walk over to the back of the wagon. Emma helps Abigail into the back of the wagon. Emma hears a horse behind her and notices Abigail staring at something. Emma reaches up into the wagon, grabs her double barreled shotgun and quickly swings around and points it at...

Cole, who is on horseback near them. Emma cocks both hammers back. "STOP RIGHT THERE MISTER." She yells in a deep a voice as she can muster.

Mr. Taggert hands the reins to Mrs. Taggert, then he reaches under his seat and brings up a rifle. He swings around and points the rifle at Cole. "I got's yore back Emma"

With out taking her eyes off Cole, Emma turns her head slightly, just enough so that Mr. Taggert can see her nod. "Thank you Mister Taggert."

Emma focuses all of her attention back on Cole. "We've had enough trouble for one day Mister, if n' ya even twitch I'm gonna blow ya clean off a' that hoss."

Cole now has his hands out to the side with palms facing Emma. Cole calmly replies in a soft voice. "I don't mean ya no harm, ma'am."

Mr. Taggert with a look of relief on his face, lowers his rifle. Emma's not taking any chances, she's lost to much already. She continues to point the shotgun at Cole. "What business ya have here abouts?"

"I'm trackin' the men that murdered my family and from the looks of things I'd reckon they're the same ones that did this."

"Yankee soldiers with faded blues?" Emma asks.

"Yes Ma'am that's them."

Cole motions toward the shotgun with his head. "Now if n' ya don't mind, I'd appreciate ya lowering that scatter gun, it's making me a might uncomfortable and my arms are gettin' a' bit tired too."

Emma is still a bit unsure, so she probes for more information. "Ya aimin' ta kill those men?"

"Yes, Ma'am." Cole answers with out hesitation.

"Ya got no ill will toward us?" Emma asks.

Cole shakes his head. "No, Ma'am."

Emma seems eased by Cole's answers and lowers the shotgun and smiles at him. "Alright then."

Cole relaxes his arms and smiles back.

Emma puts the shotgun back in the wagon. "I'm sorry for that I'm still a little skittish. Whats yore name?"

Cole smiles and responds. "Ya don't have ta apologize for protectin' yore family ma'am. I understand and take no offense. My names Cole, Cole Hawkins."

Emma is glad that Cole does not take offense to her actions. She thinks he looks like a decent and kind man. "Pleased ta meet ya, Mr. Hawkins. I'm Emma Jackson."

Emma pats Abigail on the leg and says, "This is my little one Abigail, The two in the wagon are Mr. and Mrs. Taggert."

Emma pauses a bit to control her emotions before continuing. "The graves belong to my husband Isiah and his Pa, Noah. Those yanks killed em' both for no reason a' tawl."

Cole leans forward in the saddle with a sympathetic look. "I'm sorry for yore loss, ma'am, I truly am and I know it don't ease the pain none but,

I can assure you, the men who done it are gonna pay."

Emma nods. "It's a little bit of a comfort to know that Mr. Hawkins, thank you."

Emma thinks to herself that although Cole looks very kind and decent on the outside, there is something strong about him. She knows that Cole would be very capable of holding his on, if it came to it. Emma points to the south. "It appears they was headed for Lamont, they're several hours ahead of ya but if n' ya ride hard, ya might catch up in a day, maybe less."

Cole tugs down on the front of his hat. "Much obliged, ma'am."

Emma nods her head, then points toward Cole's Knife. "Ya any good with that pig sticker?" she asks.

"I git by, ma'am." Cole replies.

Emma looks almost ashamed of what she says next. "I don't want ya ta think I'm some evil woman or that I take life and death lightly and I don't want ya puttin' yore self at any extra risk, but seein' how yore goin' after em' any how,"

Emma ducks her head in shame, then continues. "Well, if the opportunity presents itself I would appreciate ya usin' that on the two men with those long blades, they's the ones that killed my Isiah."

Emma slightly looks up still to embarrassed to look Cole in the eyes. "I'm sorry ta sound so disrespectful"

Cole smiles. "I understand exactly how ya feel ma'am, and I got nuthin' but respect for ya. I give ya my word, if I get the chance, they'll know what it feels like ta be stuck."

Emma does not feel shame any more and she knows just as she had thought earlier, Cole is a kind and decent man. "Thank you, Mister Hawkins and ride safe."

Cole nods once and says, "Yes ma'am, thank *you* and good luck to ya. *"*

Cole rides off in the direction of Lamont. Abigail stands up in the back of the wagon and waves good bye.

Night time...

Somewhere between the town of Lamont and the Jackson homestead. Two young cowboys, sit at a camp fire, leaning back against saddles and talking. No one around these parts know what their real names are, but they answer to Cob and Packy. Both are slender and in their early teens. "When we get back home I'm gonna ask Shelly Ann to go to the founders day dance with me." Cob says.

Packy smiles and replies. "I bet she says yes. I think she's sweet on ya."

Cob gets excited and starts to ask "Ya really think..."

He stops mid sentence. Excitement turns to fear and he looks out into the dark like he heard something. "Did ja' hear that Packy?"

Packy sits up and listens for a little bit. "No, I didn't hear nuthin'."

Cob strains to see past the camp fire into the dark. Munroe walks out of the darkness on foot.

Startled, Both young cowboys quickly jump to their feet. "Easy there boys. I didn't mean to sneak up on ya." Munroe says.

Seeing the uniform, the young cowboys relax and breath a sigh of relief and sit back down. They were raised to trust the army. Cob is the first to speak up. "It's okay sir. Ya just caught us off guard, is all. Come on in and have a seat by the fire."

Munroe walks over and has a seat on a stump near the fire. "I came in alone so that we wouldn't scare you boys half to death but, I got ten more men out there in the dark. Do you mind if they Come in?"

Cob is surprised he didn't hear that many men sooner. He's usually very observant. You have to be this far west. "Um, No Sir, bring em' on in." Cob answers.

With out anyone saying or doing anything, the men of the Hatchet start to come in out of the dark from all directions. The two young cowboys look at each other with a little worry. The two cowboys don't understand why these men had them surrounded.

Munroe notices their fear and takes pleasure in it. "Don't worry about them they was just near by to cover me. We didn't know who you were. You could have been cold blooded killers."

The men of the Hatchet try to hide their laughs. Munroe smiles with that crooked smile and continues. "What are you boys doing out here any way."

Cob calms down a bit and answers. "We're with

Mr. Applewood's cattle drive, they sent us to look for strays." "What about y'all sir, are y'all soldiers?"

Munroe nods proudly. "Yes we are, son, yes we are. We are what is called a Dragoon. Do you know what that is?"

Packy gets excited and finally speaks. "Golly yes, we learned about Dragoons last year in school. Y'all boys know how ta whoop yore enemies two ways ta Sundy." "Are ya out here looking for injuns?"

Munroe leans back and pats the tomahawk tucked into his gun-belt. "We're looking for all kinds of savages, boy." "I want to thank both of you for your kindness in sharing your fire with a bunch of old soldiers like us."

Cob nods and says, "It's our pleasure Sir. Side's mama always says that good ole southern hospitality aren't a' not be wasted."

At the sound of those words, Munroe's demeanor gets a little more frigid. "You boys are from the south?"

The two cowboys do not notice the change , they have let their guards down and believe they can trust these men. "Well we've lived just over yonder aways, near Possum Springs since we were born." Cob says has he points to the west. "But, our ma and pa are originally from Tennessee."

Munroe nods and looks at his men. "Tennessee uh? Well me and my men know how to repay southern hospitality from Tennessean offspring."

The Hatchet all smile at this statement. Munroe smiles at the two young cowboys and they smile back oblivious to what's coming next.

Early the next morning...

Cole rides into the young cowboys camp and dismounts from his horse. He looks around the camp and spots the young cowboys saddles with blood splattered all over them. Cole bends down and touches the blood to check it, he rubs it between his fingers and shakes his head. "Who'd ya kill now, ya murderin' bastards?" He mumbles to himself.

Cole stands back up and walks away from the smoldering camp fire. He looks around the area for signs of the Hatchet's direction of travel. Leading out of the camp, he spots what appears to be two separate drag marks. He remounts his horse and rides out following the drag marks.

Farther up ahead...

The Hatchet ride along a trail, leading through a mountain pass. Emmett and Red are each dragging a body behind their horses. The two young cowboys bodies are now torn and battered, they are almost unrecognizable. They have been dead for the last few miles. Only God knows the torment they went through before their deaths.

Munroe looks up to see several vultures flying overhead. "EMMETT! RED!" He yells.

Emmett and Red both look at Munroe to hear him out. "You two drag those bodies up that hill and cut em' lose, they can feed the buzzards. They're starting to stink and I don't want to smell em'."

Without saying a word, Emmett and Red ride up the hill, dragging the bodies, until they're out of sight. Buck comes riding up the trail fast from behind and rides up to Munroe. "Somebodies trailing us Colonel."

"Can ya tell who they are?" Munroe asks.

"No Sir."

"How many are there?" Munroe asks.

"Appears to just be the one." Buck replies.

Munroe ponders a bit then says, "Probably some damn bounty killer got up enough courage to come after the reward on our heads."

He looks at Buck. "Can you handle it?"

Buck flashes a conceited smile and replies. "Yes Sir, without even breaking a sweat."

Munroe nods. "Then go do it. We'll meet up with you in Lamont."

"Yes Sir, I won't be long." Buck says as he turns his horse and gallops back the way he came.

Chapter 11
Northern Thunders Mutter

A little ways back...

At the west end of the mountain pass, Cole has made up a lot of ground and has closed the distance between himself and the Hatchet. Cole with head down looking at the trail, rides after the Hatchet, when he passes a big boulder he stops his horse and dismounts. He squats down and places his hand on the ground, examining it for sign.

Cole looks up, turns his head to the side and then to the other side, he knows somethings wrong. In one fluid motion Cole stands, turns, draws, cocks and points his gun at Buck, who is standing in the trail with his gun pointed at Cole. "Whoa! Your pretty good mister." Buck says.

Buck gets a better look and he realizes it's Cole.

Buck smiles and shakes his head. "It's you! How in the hell did you survive?"

Cole does not respond. "Don't you have anything to say to an old friend?" Buck asks.

Still no response from Cole. "Now I don't remember us cutting your tongue out." Buck says.

Cole continues to stare down the barrel of his revolver with out a sound. Buck still has that cocky smile on his face, when he slightly shakes the revolver, he's pointing at Cole. "Oh well." "What are we going to do now looks like we got our selves an old fashioned Mexican stand-off."

Cole tightens his aim and speaks. "I ain't no Mexican."

Buck's smile turns to fear when he realizes to late what's going to happen. "Oh shi..." A loud BANG echoes through the pass, as Cole drops the hammer.

At the east end of the mountain pass...
The shot can still be heard, echoing in the distance. Munroe stops his horse when he hears it and listens for a bit. Munroe hears no other shots, he smiles and nudges his horse back into motion. "Buck must have got him boys. Let's get to Lamont and wet our whistles."

A short time later...
Ten members of the Hatchet approach the west end of a small town, they ride past a sign that reads, "*Welcome to Lamont, a friendly community.*" The word "*friendly*" has been scratched out and someone has scratched the word "*cowardly*" just

underneath it.

Lamont, is a typical small western town, the first building on this end of town is The Sheriff's office. As the hatchet ride by Munroe looks over to see, Sheriff Boyd Cooper, a heavy set alcoholic in his fifties, leaning against the post out side his office.

Munroe looks at Sheriff Cooper and tips his hat to him. "Hello, Boyd."

Munroe, then addresses the Hatchet. "Look here boys the famous Sheriff Boyd Cooper has come out to welcome us back to town."

The men of the Hatchet laugh, as Sheriff Cooper ducks his head, turns and walks into his office. Munroe takes pleasure when men fear him, it is always a pleasure for him to see Sheriff Cooper. The Hatchet continue on toward the saloon, just up the street.

Inside the saloon...

The "*Pig's Pride Saloon*" is a typical western saloon, there is several patrons sitting at tables. Four individuals sit at the corner table playing cards.

Slim Potts, a slender man in his late twenties, is sitting with his back to the Hatchet.

Matt Stall, is the dealer in this game, he has an average build and is in his late twenties, he is sitting to the right of Slim.

Bob "Stubby" Stubs, is a short, heavy set older man in his late forties with a scraggly beard, he is sitting directly across from Slim.

Hank Tillman, is the youngest of this bunch, in his early twenties with a muscular build, he is sitting directly across from Matt.

The ten members of the Hatchet, that are present are bellied up to the bar drinking whiskey. Slim starts to sing. "I wish I was in the land of cotton, old times there are not forgotten, look away, look away, look away, Dixie land."

Hearing this, Munroe looks up with an angry expression, then looks at the other members of the Hatchet. All the men of the Hatchet turn around and face the table with the card players.

"Are ya gonna sing or play cards?" Matt asks.

"I reckon I'm fixin' ta do both. I like that song and it helps me think, so stop naggin' at me and give me one." Slim says, as he throws down one card.

Matt deals him one more card and deals himself three.

"That's all you two do is fuss at each other like a couple a' jealous girls. Give me two cards." Stubby says, as he tosses two cards toward Matt.

Matt deals him two more cards.

"I ain't got shit, I fold." Hank says and throws his entire hand on the table, then leans back in his chair with a disappointed look on his face.

Slim continues to sing. "Southerns, hear your country call you."

Every member of the Hatchet pull a revolver and point them at the card players. The card players do not notice and continue to play. The other patrons notice and scramble to get out of the way. Unaware of the danger Slim continues his song. "Up! lest worse than death befall you! Hear the northern thunders mutter!..."

A loud roar fills the saloon, as the Hatchet open fire and empty their revolvers into the card players. The card players never see it coming, they slump and fall. They die without the chance to defend them selves. "I always hated that song." Munroe says.

The rest of the Hatchet laugh and all turn and belly back up to the bar. One of the saloon patrons Cletus Callaway , a scrawny, rotted toothed old man with a slight limp, runs out of the swinging front doors.

"Give us another bottle Dan." Munroe says.

Dan Pine, a big burly man of a bartender, Hands Munroe another whiskey bottle. Munroe holds up the bottle, then starts filling the Hatchet's glasses. He spills as much on the bar as he gets in the glasses. Munroe turns the bottle up and guzzles down what doesn't run out his mouth. Dan thinks to himself that the Pig's Pride Saloon would be a very appropriate name, if it was named after Colonel Munroe Brody.

Outside...

Cletus is now Standing outside the Sheriff's office, breathing heavy from his run. "SHERIFF." "SHERIFF COOPER." Cletus yells.

Sheriff Cooper comes out of the Sheriff's office carrying a bottle of whiskey. "What is it?" "Can't ya see I'm busy?"

"Sheriff there's been a murder in the saloon, ya have ta' come quick." Cletus pleads.

Sheriff Cooper looks at him with an empty look

like he doesn't know what to do.

"Sheriff?" "Sheriff, peoples been killed, Ya have ta get over there and do yore job." Cletus says.

"Ah hell! Okay, okay I'm comin'." Sheriff Cooper says, as he sets his bottle down on the porch and heads over to the saloon.

A short time later...

Inside the Pig's Pride Saloon, Sheriff Cooper walks in and sees the dead men, then looks over and sees the Hatchet leaning against the bar and smiling at him. Sheriff Cooper tries to avoid eye contact with the Hatchet, as he walks over to the bar. "Give me a shot Dan." The Sheriff mumbles.

Dan is reluctant and tries to dissuade the Sheriff. "Sheriff, maybe..."

"GIVE ME A GAWD DAMN SHOT DAN." Sheriff Cooper interrupts.

Dan disgusted, turns over a glass and slams it on the bar in front of Sheriff Cooper, then pours him a drink. Sheriff Cooper quickly knocks it back and turns away from the bar. "Somebody clean this mess up." Sheriff Cooper says as he lazily motions at the dead men lying on the floor.

"Take the bodies over to the undertaker and tell em' I said ta take care of it." He says.

Some of the patrons start gathering the bodies and carrying them out. Still avoiding eye contact Sheriff Cooper heads for the swinging doors of the saloon.

"HEY, BOYD." Munroe yells.

Sheriff cooper stops midway out the door but

does not turn around. He's so scared that he's shaking.

"You have a good day, Boyd. It was good seeing you again." Munroe says.

The Hatchet laugh, as Sheriff Cooper ducks his head and continues on out. "Well boys I believe we had enough fun, it's time we headed out." Munroe says.

"Sergeant." Munroe addresses Jack.

"Yes, sir." Jack answers, as he walks over to Munroe.

"Buck should have been back by now." "I want you, your brother and skinner to wait here for him a little longer." Munroe says.

"Yes sir, Colonel." Jack says.

Jack motions for Jake and Skinner, all three go sit at a table.

"DAN." Munroe yells.

Startled Dan jumps, he hates that deep, bellowing voice. Dan walks to the end of the bar near Munroe. "Yes sir, Colonel Brody, what can I do for ya?"

"We're going to need some wet goods to take with us. Can you fix us up?" Munroe poses it as a question, but everyone that hears it knows it's a demand.

Dan knows something bad would happen, if he were to refuse. "Um, Yes sir. I just got a fresh supply this mornin'. You go around back Bob will load ya up."

Munroe flashes Dan a dominating smile. "Thank you, Dan."

Munroe then turns to face Skinner. "SKINNER."
He yells.

Skinner looks up and listens.

"Before you head out, you take the wagon
around back and load up some wet goods and bring
em' with you." Munroe says.

"Yes sir!" Skinner says.

Skinner turns and rejoins Jack and Jake at the
table.

"Let's ride men." Munroe says.

The six other members of the Hatchet follow
Munroe out the door.

Outside...

Just as the seven members of the Hatchet walk
out of the Pig's Pride Saloon, Hanna Jenkins, a
petite, intelligent looking school teacher in her
twenties and one of her students Billy Haskell, a
husky little boy around ten years old, walk by.

Billy is not an orphan, he has a father, if you can
call him that. Everyone else simply calls him no
account or nothing. His father never is around much
except to beat Billy every now and then. So Billy
avoids him as much as possible. Because of this
Hanna has taken it up on herself to look out for
Billy. Of coarse if you asked Billy, it's him that
looks after Miss Jenkins. The truth is they both look
out for each other.

Munroe sees Hanna and smiles. Hanna is one of
those women that are hard to miss. She is intelligent
looking, but she is also very attractive. Then again it
wouldn't have mattered one way or the other to

Munroe. He'll take them anyway he can get them.

"Well hello there little lady. How bout you come up here and give me a kiss?" Munroe asks.

Hanna ignores Munroe but, Billy stops and gives him a mean look. Billy is young enough to still have the courage that most men around here have lost. He knows what the Hatchet are, but he is not a bit afraid. "Ya don't talk ta her mister. Ya ain't nuthin' but a murderin' peace of scum."

Hanna grabs Billy by the arm but he's determined to be heard and resists. "Billy don't tempt them, these men are capable of anything." Hanna says.

"You better listen to your Mama boy. You got gumption but, if you keep wagging that tongue like that someone might cut it out." Munroe says.

"She ain't my Mama and I ain't skeared a' you mister." Billy says.

A small crowd of towns people have now gathered, to watch. Billy addresses his next questions to them. "What's wrong with everybody are ya jus' gonna let them ride in, kill people and then ride back out, whenever they please? Ain't anybody gonna do nuthin'?"

Munroe draws his knife and points it at Billy. "That's exactly what they're going to do boy, *Nothing.*"

Monroe raises his knife and licks the blade. "Now, show me that sharp tongue of yours boy, we'll see what cuts deeper, your tongue or my blade."

"LET'S GO BILLY." Hanna yells.

She pulls on Billy's arm, but he won't budge. "BILLY DON HASKELL, YOU GET MOVING RIGHT THIS INSTANT." Hanna screams.

She pulls on Billy's arm one more time and finally gets him moving. There's something about using a boy's full name that gets him motivated. It's as though they respond to it from instinct. Billy stomps off angry and disappointed. "I hate this town, there ain't nuthin' but a bunch of cowards here. I'm ashamed ta even live here."

Billy turns around for one more out burst. "YA HEAR ME I'M ASHAMED OF EVERYONE OF YA."

Billy then turns once again to stomp along side Hanna.

"Feel better?" Hanna asks.

"No ma'am." Billy replies.

He's still stewing over the events. Hanna relaxes and smiles, knowing they are far enough away to be safe. "It'll get better one day Billy" "I mean it's got to, it can not get any worse. Right?" Hanna asks.

Billy shrugs his shoulders. "If you say so Miss Jenkins" Billy says.

He hopes his teacher is right, but even at only ten years old, Billy Haskell has just about run out of hope.

Munroe sheaths his knife and watches Billy and Hanna walk away until they are out of sight. Munroe's eyes glaze over as he thinks of the evil things he should have done to them. Then he snaps back to reality. "Boots and saddles." he says as he motions to the horses.

The seven Hatchet men mount up and ride out of town.

Chapter 12
The Blurred Badge

Later...

Inside the Pig's Pride Saloon, Jack, Jake and Skinner are sitting at a table playing cards. Jack throws his cards on the table and leans back in his chair. "I'm tired of all this waiting around. Buck should a' been here by now. Hell, he may be fiddle assin' around out there while we're sittin' here wasting time."

"You think something might of happened to him?" Jake asks.

"I don't know but, I'm through waiting. Jake you go saddle the horses and bring em' back here. Skinner you go out back and see if they got the whiskey loaded, bring the wagon back around and we'll ride back together and see what the Colonel wants us to do." Jack says.

Skinner nods his head, stands and heads out the back. Jake stands and walks over to the bar, he looks in the mirror behind the bar and straightens his hat and admires himself a bit, then turns and heads for the door. "See ya next time, Dan." Jake says as he exits through the swinging doors.

Dan looks up just long enough to shake his head in disgust.

Around this same time...

On the outskirts of town, Cole is riding into Lamont. He looks up and watches a hawk flying over head. Doc Boon, a snake oil salesman, fancy dressed and driving an enclosed box wagon being pulled by two mules, is headed out of town.

The words, "*Doc Boon's Miracle Elixir*", is painted on the side of the wagon in big letters. Under this in smaller letters it reads, "*A cure all for body and soul*."

Doc Boon sees Cole looking up at the sky. "The lord looks down on us all brother." Doc says.

Cole looks at the Salesman, With a cold expression. "Well, Snake Oil, if he is, he ain't gonna like what he sees from neither of *us*."

Doc Boon is both confused and offended, he slaps the reins on his mules and continues on down the road. Cole smiles and heads on into Lamont.

Just up the street aways...

Jake is standing on the boardwalk of the Pig's Pride Saloon, looking toward the edge of town. He takes a second look when he sees Cole. He stares close to make sure it's Cole. Jake watches Cole get off his horse in front of the Sheriff's Office. Cole wraps the reins once around the hitching post and walks into the Sheriff's Office.

"I'll be damned." Jake thinks to himself as he quickly turns and reenters the saloon.

Inside the Pig's Pride Saloon...
Jack looks up to see Jake come back in. "You back already?" Jack asks.

"I never got a chance ta leave, ya ain't gonna believe who I just saw walk into the Sheriff's office." Jake says.

Jack leans forward interested as Jake smiles big, nods and starts telling his story.

Inside the Sheriff's office...
Sheriff Cooper is leaning back in his chair with his feet on his desk taking a swig from a whiskey bottle. He hasn't noticed that Cole is standing by the door. Cole slams the door shut, to announce his presence. Startled Sheriff Cooper almost falls backward and chokes on his drink. He quickly puts his feet on the floor and sets up.

"Yes sir, what can I do for ya?" Sheriff Cooper manages to asks between coughs as he tries not to drown on the whiskey he just swallowed.

"Sheriff, my names Cole Hawkins, I need ta report some murders done by a group of men calling themselves the Hatchet."

Sheriff Cooper starts to wonder if it would have

been better to of drowned on the whiskey. "Yea, I know of em'." "What about em'?" he asks.

Cole moves closer to the desk. They murdered my family and a few others. I'm goin' after em'." Cole says.

"Was wonderin' if ya wanted ta ride a' long?" Cole asks.

Sheriff Cooper takes a big swig from the bottle, then wipes his mouth with his sleeve. "Nah, I reckon I want ta go on livin' for a bit longer."

Cole doesn't understand why a man that wears that badge, won't honor it. "They're murderers, Sheriff. It's your job ta stop em'."

Sheriff Cooper doesn't respond and avoids eye contact.

"What if they come here?" Cole asks.

Sheriff Cooper ducks his head and wipes his mouth with his hand. "They already have." He says quietly.

"What?" Cole asks, not sure that he heard the sheriff right.

Sheriff Cooper slightly raises his head but is too ashamed to look Cole in the eyes. "They already been here, more than once and they kill someone every time, but I can't do nuthin' there's to many of em' and they're trained soldiers."

Sheriff Cooper is trying to convince Cole and himself that doing nothing is the right thing to do. It may be easy to convince himself, but he will never convince Cole.

Sheriff Cooper looks up, but only makes eye contact briefly, before looking away again. "You can't stop em' either. You won't survive against men like that. It's best you just leave it be and forget about it." Sheriff cooper says.

Cole, angry, places both hands on Sheriff Coopers desk and leans closer toward him. Forget it? FORGET IT? My wife was raped and tortured by thirteen men. My little girl was skinned and the man that done it took her little ear as a keep sake. I'll never forget that. NEVER."

Sheriff Cooper leans back in his chair with a look of fear on his face. He didn't think anyone could make him feel fear more than Colonel Munroe Brody, but Cole Hawkins just has.

Cole calms his voice just a bit and continues. "As far as survivin', I buried the man I was, with my family, I got nuthin' left ta lose. Doesn't matter whether I live or not, I'm gonna kill as many of them bastards as I can before I go. With yore help we might be able ta git a few more."

Sheriff Cooper shakes his head no as he ducks it in shame. Cole is now more disgusted than angry. "Ya took an oath ta uphold law and order and ta do everything in yore power ta stop men like this."

Sheriff Cooper takes another swig and finds a little courage in the bottle, and sets back up in his chair. "THAT OATH DON'T MEAN SHIT IF I'M DEAD." Sheriff Cooper yells.

He sees Cole squint and the fear creeps back in and he lowers his voice. "There's too many of em' we can't get em' all."

Cole stands back up straight, taking his hands off the desk. "Ya don't have ta get em' all. If every man they went up against would just git one or two, it would soon end and countless lives would be saved."

"Not all men that wear a tin star are heroes." Sheriff Cooper says.

Cole shakes his head in disgust. "Yea and not all men that wear it, earn it. Ya don't have ta be a hero, Sheriff ya just need ta do yore job."

Sheriff Cooper looks at the half empty bottle of whiskey. "Dying ain't much of a job."

Cole is tired of wasting time trying to convince the Sheriff to do his job. "FINE. If yore too much of a' drunk, coward ta do yore job, then I'll go it alone. But, I'll tell ya now Sheriff, don't git in my way or try an stop me, cause yore so liquored up that, that badge is startin' ta blur."

"There's papers on every member of that gang, wanted dead or alive. Not only will I not stand in yore way, but I'll pay ya the bounty if ya succeed." Sheriff Cooper says.

"Hell! I'll even go ya one further, if ya accomplish what yore settin' out ta do, I'll give up this damn badge." Sheriff Cooper says, as he leans back in his chair and crosses his arms.

"Now, if ya don't mind, I don't like jawin' with dead men." He adds.

Cole leans forward a little with a serious look on his face. "Ya best git ready for retirement Sheriff, cause those boys have done got me riled and they ain't gonna like it, and neither are you."

Cole turns and heads for the door.

Chapter 13
Live By the Blade Die By the Blade

Outside...

Cole walks out of the Sheriff's Office and looks up to see Jack and Jake standing on the other side of the street in front of him. Jack nudges Jake with his elbow. "Lookee here Jake, ole Cole crawled out of the depths of hell to hunt us down, just like he said he would."

Jake smiles at Cole. "I thought we killed you Cole?"

"I reckon ya did a piss poor job of it." Cole answers calm and confident.

Jack and Jake stand side by side and square off to Cole. Cole moves his right hand near the *Remington Outlaw* holstered in the strong draw position. Cole wiggles his fingers to get Jack and

Jake's attention, when they glance at his right hand, Cole sneaks his left hand around his back and grips the *Remington Frontier* tucked in at the small of his back. Cole has no false illusions about this being a fair and honorable fight. He knows his only chance is to draw the revolver, from behind his back and the one at his side, at the same time. If he can manage this he can kill both opponents, before they kill him.

Sheriff Cooper comes out of his office and sees Cole facing off against Jack and Jake. Sheriff cooper quickly steps to the side to get out of the line of fire. Cole knows he can not count on this coward to back him up.

Something catches Cole's attention, he glances up the street and sees Emma and Abigail Jackson getting on the stage. Emma nods her head at Cole then steps up into the stage. Cole looks down at his knife, releases his grip on the *Frontier* and holds both hands slightly out to his sides with palms facing forward.

"You giving up Cole?" Jack asks.

"Sheriff take the revolver out of my waist band." Cole says.

Sheriff cooper walks over to Cole. The sheriff confused starts to ask "What are ya..."

"JUST DO IT." Cole interrupts, He doesn't have time to explain.

Sheriff Cooper removes the *Remington Frontier* from the small of Cole's back. With his left hand Cole unfastens his gun belt and hands it to Sheriff Cooper.

"It's good you gave up Cole, you wouldn't have beaten us anyway." Jack says.

"I ain't givin' up. jus' wanna kill you boys in the manner ya deserve." Cole says.

Cole puts his right thumb in his knife lanyard wraps it around his hand and grips the knife in a saber grip and unsheathes it. "Live by the blade, die by the blade. What a' ya say boys, ya wanna give it a go?"

Both brothers seem pleased. They would choose sabers over guns any day of the week. "You got sand Cole. Hell yea, we'll give it a go." Jack says.

Jack and Jake draw their sabers with their right hands and step out into the street.

"Ya done gone plum loco, Hawkins?" Sheriff Cooper asks.

"Just shoot em', they'll cut ya ta pieces. Them boys where born with them blades. Hell, some say they weren't born a' tawl, they just cut their way out of their mama's womb with them big pig stickers." Sheriff Cooper says.

Cole steps out into the street to face off against Jack and Jake. Jake looks at Cole's knife, then holds up his saber. "Ours are bigger, Cole."

"It ain't the size of the blade that matters, it's where ya stick it that counts." Cole says.

All three men are in constant motion, Jack and Jake try to find a position of attack and Cole is trying to keep the brothers lined up so that they can not attack at the same time.

Jack thrusts his saber at Cole's midsection, Cole steps slightly to the side and forward and grabs

Jack's wrist with his left hand. Cole then quickly thrusts his own knife toward Jack's midsection, Jack grabs Cole's wrist with his free hand and the two men struggle.

Cole glances over to see Jake trying to move into a position to Cole's right side. Cole pushes his arms forward to make room, then front kicks Jack, knocking him to the ground.

Jake thrusts his saber at Cole's side, Cole hollows out, narrowly avoiding a stab. Cole grabs Jake's wrist with his left hand as it passes by. Then quickly in fluid motions smashes his right elbow into Jake's face twice. WHAM! WHAM! Then Cole quickly extends his arm slashing his knife toward Jake's throat.

Jake rapidly jerks his head back and avoids getting his throat cut but, stumbles backward and falls to the ground. Jack and Jake both quickly jump to their feet. Once again the three men start circling each other. Jack and Jake both thought this would be an easy victory. They were wrong, they now know that When Cole is not cooperating, he stops being an easy victim and becomes a savage opponent.

"Your good Cole, but I'm through playing around. I got your rhythm now." Jack says.

Jack slashes at Cole's midsection, Cole hollows out as the saber blade passes close by. With out pause Jack swings the saber back toward Cole's neck.

Cole quickly ducks, narrowly avoiding contact with the blade. Jake thrusts toward Cole's face, Cole quickly steps and shifts as the blade grazes his cheek drawing blood. Cole maneuvers himself around to line Jack and Jake back up.

Jack thrusts at Cole's midsection once more and again Cole shifts and steps in avoiding the blade and grabs Jack's wrist. Cole responds yet again by thrusting his knife at Jack's midsection and as before Jack hollows out and grabs Cole's wrist.

The two men again struggle but this time Jack pulls his arms and Cole forward and head butts Cole in the face. Cole's head snaps back and he staggers backward and shuffles his feet to remain standing. Cole now has blood seeping down his nicked cheek and running out his busted nose.

Jack gets cocky again, he believes he has already won. "I want to let you know Cole, that when everyone was taking turns with your wife, Me and Jake done her together. In spite of all the screaming and carrying on, I think she enjoyed it."

Cole is now truly and noticeably Pissed, but he also knows that Jack wants him to loose control. If he rushes in, in a blind rage he would be easy prey for the two experienced killers. Jacks taunt won't work, Cole will use the anger and channel it into energy and motion. Instead of rushing in blindly, Cole will instead do some experienced killing of his own.

Cole using the lanyard swings his knife from a saber grip into a reverse grip. This grip is not very common in this day and age and it just might give Cole the edge he needs. "If you an yore brother like doing things together, then ya can die an go ta hell with each other." Cole says.

Jack Swings his saber towards Cole's left side, Cole steps in and blocks Jacks forearm with a left outside down block and with the now reversed gripped knife, slashes Jack's throat. Cole starts to spin around to the left as he throws Jack's body to the ground. He moves with great skill and grace.

Cole continues to spin, as Jake swings his saber in a downward slash from overhead, toward Cole's head. Cole now has spun all the way around, steps in and blocks Jake's saber arm with a left rising block. In a fluid motion Cole buries his knife to the hilt into Jake's clavicle notch.

"AAAGGGHHH!" Jake screams in pain and drops to his knees.

With his left hand, Cole grabs Jake's hair and pushes his head back. In another fluid motion Cole pulls the knife out of the clavicle notch, runs the blade across Jake's neck and knees him in the chest, knocking Jake to the ground.

That makes three, there's ten left and Cole Hawkins always finishes what he starts. The Hatchet have ruled this part of the west with a rein of terror since the end of the Civil War. That's to long and if Cole has anything to say about that rein of terror will end very soon. He is now off to a decent start.

Chapter 14
An Understanding

Up the street to the east...

Inside the general store, Hanna puts some goods on the counter as billy stands looking at candy. Behind the counter is the store clerk, Mr. Peavey, a tall, lanky man with thick bottle cap glasses. No one knows his first name, just Mr. Peavey. Some folks even think Mister might just be his first name. Mister Peavey is the solemn type, he never laughs and rarely smiles. In spite of this he is friendly and most folks like him.

"Will that be all Miss Jenkins?" Mr. Peavey asks.

Hanna smiles warmly and starts to ask a question. "Mister Peavey do have any..."

Before Hanna can finish her statement, Cletus runs into the General Store yelling. "HE DID IT.

HE KILLED'EM BOTH."

"Who done what to who?" Mr. Peavey asks in a solemn voice.

Cletus struggles to catch his breath.

"Calm down Cletus and tell us what's going on." Mr. Peavey says.

Still gasping for air Cletus tries to speak. "A stranger... he cut down the... Farley brothers... using only a knife." Cletus manages to gasp out between breaths.

"The Farley brothers from the Hatchet?" Mr. Peavey asks.

Cletus still trying to catch his breath simply nods his head.

"Using only a Knife?" Mr. Peavey asks.

Cletus, still breathing heavy, nods his head again.

"I gotta see this." Billy says, as he runs out the door.

Hanna tries to grab him, but misses. "BILLY HASKELL, YOU STOP RIGHT THIS INSTANT." Hanna yells.

Billy pays her no mind and continues on his way. First and last name doesn't quite have the same effect on little boys as their full name does.

"I'll be back for these Mister Peavey." Hanna says.

"That's fine, I'm coming too." Mr. Peavey says.

He hasn't been this excited in years, maybe never. Hanna rushes out the door, Mr. Peavey comes from around the counter and is right behind her. Both run past Cletus who is still out of breath.

Cletus looks around to see he is alone. He

111

brushes them off with a wave toward the door. He looks around and grabs a bucket. He sits on the bucket to exhausted to do anything else.

Back at the west end of town...

Billy comes running down the street to where Cole and sheriff Cooper are. Cole is strapping his holster back on. Billy looks on eyes wide with excitement. "Golly gosh darn, it's true. It's about time someone stood up ta them an gave em' what for."

Hanna and Mr. Peavey come running down the street shortly behind Billy. Hanna grabs billy and covers his eyes. "You don't need to see such vulgarism."

"Ah gee whiz, Miss Jenkins, It's the only thing ta see in Lamont." Billy says.

Sheriff Cooper hands Cole the Remington Frontier and Cole Tucks it back in at the small of his back. "What now Cole?" Sheriff Cooper asks.

"Nothin's changed, I'm still goin' after the rest of em'." Cole answers.

Hanna, hearing Cole's response, let's go of Billy and approaches Cole. "You planning on killing them, Mister?" Hanna asks.

"Yes ma'am." Cole says without hesitation.

"Your no better than they are. You have no right to decide who lives or who dies." Hanna says.

"After what they done, I'm makein' it my right." Cole responds.

"It does not matter what they have done, two wrongs does not make a right, Mister." Hanna says.

112

Cole flashes Hanna an angry look. "It matters ta me."

He then composes himself and looks her up and down. "You a school marm, ma'am?"

"A teacher, yes and it's miss Jenkins." Hanna says.

"Well Miss Jenkins do ya teach number addin'?" Cole asks.

"Arithmetic, yes I do." Hanna answers.

"Well, Miss Jenkins when ya add two odd numbers do they come out even?" Cole asks.

Hanna is a little confused by Cole's questions. "Yes but, I do not see what your getting at Mister?"

"What I'm gettin' at ma'am, is that I don't know nor care weather two wrongs make a' right or not, but I do know that two odds make an even, and I damn well plan on gettin' even with the Hatchet." Cole says.

Hanna is now angry and opens her mouth to say something, but before see can speak her mind, Sheriff Cooper grabs her arm and starts pulling her away. "Let me go Sheriff, Those bounty killers are no better than the men they hunt." Hanna says.

"He ain't no bounty killer. Now come here and I'll explain." Sheriff Cooper says, as he continues to drag Hanna by the arm.

After Sheriff Cooper gets Hanna a ways back, he explains Cole's situation.

No one can hear what he is saying but, it is obvious from her expression that he is explaining What happened to Cole's family. Hanna's expression turns from anger, to shock, to disgust, to sadness and finally sympathy.

Billy walks over and lightly tugs on Hanna's sleeve and she turns to look at him. "Miss Jenkins, he's the only one willin' ta stand up ta these men. Ya said things would get better. Well, he might be the only one that can make it happen."

With an understanding look, Hanna touches Billy's cheek with her hand and smiles. Hanna walks back over to Cole. "I'm sorry Mister Hawkins, I judged you wrongly."

"I believe the way I do and you believe the way you do ma'am, there's no reason ta apologize for yore beliefs." Cole says.

"Please let me finish Mister Hawkins." Hanna says.

"Sorry ma'am, go ahead." Cole says.

"I may not agree with what your doing, but I understand why your doing it. It's a shame what some men are capable of doing and I'm sorry for your loss." Hanna says.

Cole nods a thank you, but says nothing and lets Hanna Continue. "The less monsters there are, the better this world will be. Well, what I'm trying to say is, if you do what your doing Mister Hawkins, then maybe the children I teach won't have to. So I wish you luck and please be careful." Hanna finishes with a warm smile.

Cole nods his head. "Thank ya ma'am."

Hanna doesn't normally hold to violence, but she ponders the way of the west. It is a hard and harsh land. Sometimes it can be down right cruel. She knows you can't judge a man for shooting a snake before it bites someone. You can't resent a man for putting down a rabid dog that is a danger to a community. And you can't expect good people to do nothing when wolves threaten their stock and livelihoods.

Hanna now understands that out here in the west, that some men are no different than the other feral beast. And she thinks that maybe sometimes these men have to be put down, when they become a threat to decent people. She also realizes that it is not her place to judge or resent the man that does it. And she can't expect this man to do nothing after what he has seen and been through.

Chapter 15
What Goes Around Comes Around

Down the street on the east end of town...

Skinner pulls the wagon around a building and onto the street heading for the Pig's Pride Saloon. When he sees the people standing around, he stops the wagon and strains to see what's going on.

He sees two bodies dressed in faded blues lying on the ground and he realizes Jack and Jake are dead. He scans the bystanders for a clue, then he recognizes Cole. When he see's Cole look up at him, Skinner's eyes go big with shock and fear. Skinner slaps the reins and quickly starts trying to turn the wagon around.

Cole see's the wagon and the man sitting in the seat. He would recognize this man from three times this distance, and as Munroe once remarked, you can smell him from here. Skinner now has the wagon turned around and is heading out of town as fast as he can.

Cole runs to his horse grabs his rifle out of the scabbard, aims and fires, BANG! The bullet hits the corner of a building, just as skinner passes behind it. Cole slams the rifle back into the scabbard jumps on his horse and chases after Skinner.

Billy can not contain his excitement. "GO GET EM' MISTER HAWKINS, GIVE EM' HELL."

Hanna opens her mouth in surprise. "BILLY DON HASKELL, YOU WATCH YOUR MOUTH."

Billy ducks his head, but can't keep from smiling. "Sorry Miss Jenkins, I jus' got carried away."

Cole Hawkins never thought of himself as anything special, just a normal man, who gets by. But in the eyes of Billy Haskell, Cole is larger than life. A hero that will set the world right. Without even knowing it, Cole Hawkins has just given a ten year old boy a precious gift. The gift of hope, for the first time in a long while, Billy has hope. He now truly believes what Hanna said. He feels it in his bones, things will get better and Cole Hawkins is the one who will make it better.

East of Lamont near Canton Creek...

Skinner frantically slaps the reins on his horses and looks behind him to see if Cole is still chasing him. Cole is aways back but, closing quickly. Skinner slaps the reins hard. "HAW! HAW! HAW! FASTER YOU DAMN NAGS, FASTER." Skinner yells.

Skinner's front wagon wheel hits a big rock and shatters. The wagon drops and digs into the dirt, as it breaks away from the horses. The wagon flips and throws skinner out. The wagon flips end to end with parts flying off in all directions. Whats left of it comes to a stop on it's side.

Skinner as quickly as he can stands, pulls his revolver, cocks, aims and it's to late. Cole jumps from his horse tackling Skinner, the two men hit the ground hard and Skinner's revolver is knocked away. Cole continues the momentum and rolls to his feet and turns to face Skinner. Skinner struggles to stand quickly, but without as much grace.

"We don't have ta do this, Cole." Skinner says.

"Yea we do." Cole says, as he steps back over to Skinner and Punches him hard in the face.

Skinner's head and body move with the force of the punch and Skinner staggers, but remains on his feet. Skinner rushes forward at Cole's waist to try and tackle him. Cole shifts and throws Skinner to the ground.

Skinner stands back up and pulls out his knife. "DAMN IT. I'm gonna cut out your gizzard, boy." Skinner says.

"Yore gonna try ya fat, ugly bastard, but ya ain't got the grit ta git it done." Cole says.

Skinner lunges at Cole with the knife, Cole side steps grabs Skinner's knife hand and turns to flip Skinner to the ground. As skinner stands back up, Cole kicks the knife from his hand and slams a back fist into Skinners face.

Skinner stumbles backward near the wagon, picks up a piece of wood that broke off the wagon and swings it forcefully at Cole's head. Cole catches the end of it with his left hand, then smashes it in two with his right forearm and continues to spin around to smash his half into Skinner's head. WHAM! The wood shatters on impact, Skinner spins with the force of the blow as he falls to the ground with a THUD! Cole throws the remaining piece of wood in his hand onto Skinner. Skinner is no match at all for Cole. It's clear to see that Skinner is nothing, without the rest of the Hatchet to back his play.

A short time later...

The wagon is on it's side, and Skinner is tied to the under part of it in a kneeling position, unconscious. Cole is squatting down in front of him, lightly slapping Skinner's face, with the back of his hand, to wake him. "Wake up ya piece of shit. I wouldn't want ya ta miss any of this."

Skinner awakens and lunges at Cole, but is stopped by the ropes. Skinner looks at the ropes, then back to Cole and Smiles. "Oh, am I supposed ta be scared now?"

Cole, without responding or showing any emotion, continues to look at Skinner.

"Ya know Cole, when I skinned your daughter she screamed real good." Skinner taunts.

Cole slams his fist into Skinners face, skinners head is snapped to the side and down from the force. Skinner raises his head back up blood

119

running from his mouth. Skinner spits tobacco juice on the ground, This time it's mixed with blood and teeth. "God damn, son of a bitchin', god damn. I'll give ya one thing Cole you sure can hit, feels like gettin' kicked by a damn mule."

Cole Holds Skinners knife in his right hand and runs his left thumb along the blade to check the sharpness. Skinner starts to show fear when he sees the knife. "Wha.. What are you gonna do with that?"

Cole slowly raises his head and looks at Skinner. "I'm gonna see how good ya scream."

Skinner already regrets saying what he did about Cole's daughter. "Wait..."

Skinner starts to speak, but Before he can finish, Cole grabs Skinner's left ear with his left hand and in one fluid motion cuts Skinner's ear off and Skinner screams. Skinner screams real good.

"AAAAAGGGGHHHH! GOD DAMN, SON OF A BITCH'IN GOD DAMN. SHIT, PLEASE, PLEASE, Please Cole I didn't kill your little girl, Red did, he shot her in the back. She was already dead when I got there. So when I did what I did it wasn't as bad as you thought. Your little girl didn't feel a thing."

Cole gives him a go to hell look. "You will."

Cole reaches the knife toward Skinner's right ear, as Skinner continues to scream.
"NOOOOOOOOOOOO."

They say what goes around comes around. Skinner has done a lot to many people. Now it has come back to him. Cole is not an evil man, but he does believe in an eye for an eye. Before Cole is done, Skinner will know what it feels like to be on the wrong end of that skinning knife.

An hour later...

Cole walks toward the creek still holding Skinner's knife, his hands and arms are covered in blood. His whole body is shaking, as he looks at the knife and throws it into some bushes. He drops to his hands and knees near the waters edge and looks at his reflection.

This is the worst thing he has ever done. He feels kind of sick to his stomach, but he's not ashamed of it. It needed doing, if any one man ever deserved to be tortured, it was Skinner. "They deserve everything they get and you'll do whatever ya have ta', ta' make sure they get it. Now lets finish this."

Cole washes the blood off of his hands and arms in the creek. He can't leave just yet, before Cole can head out there is something else he has to do here.

A short time later...

Cole is standing in front of what appears to be seven tiny graves. They are, he has buried the seven ears that Skinner had collected from his victims, Including Sara's ear. Cole thought it was the decent thing to do. He thought about burying Skinners body also, but decided he wasn't that decent. Besides even if he was, Skinner didn't deserve it.

Cole is standing directly in front of the spot he buried his daughters ear, holding his hat and trying to fight back the tears. "I'm sorry sweet pea. I'm sorry my past caused ya so much pain. I can't take it away and I can't make it right. The only thing I can do is make sure they can't do it to anyone else."

Cole continues to fight back the tears. "I love you Sara and I hope you and yore mama are in a place that makes ya safe and happy."

Cole put's his hat on and swallows hard, trying to swallow his feelings. He has business to finish and it's time he got to it. Cole hopes to see his family again, but he doesn't know how it will be possible. Not after what he's done and is about to do again. It doesn't matter whether you seek justice or revenge. When you take another man's life, there is always a price to pay. Cole knows he won't like the price, but he's willing to pay it just the same.

Chapter 16
One Bullet One Chance

On a hill overlooking the Hatchet's hideout...

Its late in the day now, Cole sits on his horse looking down at the hideout. He sees a wagon approaching the entrance. Cole gets off his horse and pulls a spy scope out of the saddle bags. He extends the scope, squats down and places one elbow on his knee to study the scope, then looks through it, to get a better look.

Wade and Clay are in the wagon and it is loaded with crates. There is writing on the crates. As the wagon turns and heads for the hideout, Cole can read the writing. In red paint and capital letters the writing reads "CAUTION! DYNAMITE!"

As the wagon enters through the front gate, the remaining members of the Hatchet come out to meet it. When the wagon stops Munroe walks over to it. "You boys have any problems?"

"No Sir. The bean eaters didn't give us no trouble at all." Wade answers.

"So you let em' live?" Munroe asks.

"Well Sir, I didn't exactly say that." Wade says.

The Hatchet laugh and Munroe slaps Wade on the arm. Munroe puts his hand on one of the crates. "Lets get this dynamite into the barn, men."

Munroe walks toward the house as the rest of the men start grabbing crates and carrying them to the barn.

Back on the hill...

Cole closes the scope and puts it back in the saddle bag. It's getting dark now. He unstraps the saddle cinch, removes the saddle from the horse and places it on the ground. he pulls the saddle blanket off and throws it to the side as well. Cole pats his horse on the side of the neck. "I best try ta get some sleep, looks like it's gonna be a might busy day tomorrow."

It might seem strange to some people that a man would speak to his horse this way, but out here a man forms a special bond with his horse. Without a horse a man could die wandering through this vast open land. He has to learn to trust his horse, and his horse has to trust him. They say a dog is a man's best friend. Not out here, out here a horse is a man's best friend. It seems only natural to speak to your best friend.

Early the next morning...

Cole is on the outside of the log fencing of the Hatchets Hideout, sneaking toward the entrance. Cole gets behind a wagon parked next to the fence near the entrance.

J.T. is standing on the closest side of the entrance and Wade is standing on the far side of the entrance. J.T. Grabs his crotch to indicate he has to piss. "I'm gonna go check the perimeter." J.T. Says.

"Don't pull on that thing too hard, you might pull the little thing clean off." Wade says.

Wade smiles as J.T. shakes his head in disgust and walks toward the wagon.

Cole leans against the back of the wagon and waits. As J.T. passes the wagon Cole Quickly steps in behind him, grabs J.T.'s Chin with one hand and the back of his head with the other hand, Cole kicks the back of J.T.'s knee dropping him to both knees and then with one smooth, violent motion Cole twists and snaps J.T.'s neck.

Cole doesn't have time to hide the body. Wade heard the commotion and is heading toward the wagon. "J.T. whats wrong?"

Then, Wade spots the body. "Oh shi..."

Before Wade can fully understand what's happening and raise his rifle, Cole in one smooth motion grabs his knife, pulls it from the sheath, turns and throws it at Wade.

The knife sticks deep into Wade's neck, he opens his mouth like he's trying to scream, but no sound comes out. Wade drops to his knees then falls forward face first into the dirt.

125

Cole walks over, pulls his knife from Wade's body, wipes the blade on Wade's jacket and slides it back into the sheath. Cole sneaks to the entrance. With his back pressed to the log fence, he slowly scans the inside perimeter. Cole sneaks through the entrance and heads toward the house.

On top of the barn, Clay is walking on the far side of the roof and keeping watch, as he approaches the top he can see over the top of the log fence. He can see far enough over the fence to spot Wade's body lying outside near the entrance. Clay immediately starts to scan the rest of the grounds. he spots Cole, who now has his back pressed against the house, peeking into a window.

Clay raises his rifle, aims and FIRES, his foot slips a little and he misses. The bullet strikes the side of the house near Cole's Head. Cole dives forward, away from the house rolls, pulls his revolver and FIRES. Clay is silhouetted by the sky, making him a very good target. Cole doesn't miss, the bullet strikes Clay in the chest.

Clay grabs his wound and falls forward over the peak of the roof and tumbles all the way down the front side and off. His body hits the ground hard, he never moves.

Cole turns to see Emmett come out of the house, revolver in hand. Emmett and Cole spot each other and raise their revolvers. Cole FIRES first, the bullet strikes the edge of the door frame as Emmett dives back inside.

Cole quickly turns and runs for the barn. The remaining members of the Hatchet exit the house and see Cole running. They open fire and a volley of bullets hit the walls, as Cole enters the barn. "Well, we know you boys can hit the broad side of a barn." Emmett says, as he shakes his head.

Munroe slams open the door and stomps out, buckling his gun belt. "WHAT THE HELL'S GOING ON OUT HERE?"

"It's him Colonel, he's here." Emmett says.

"Him who?" Munroe asks, with a confused look on his face.

"Damn it Emmett make some sense." Munroe says.

"Cole! Cole Hawkins. He's here. He damn near shot my head off, before running into the barn." Emmett says.

Preacher raises his bible and starts spouting. "He shall rise from the depths of hell and smite his enemy with fire and brimstone...."

Munroe grabs Preacher by the collar and pulls him face to face. "SHUT YOUR DAMN MOUTH, YOU SORRY ASS HYPOCRITE."

Munroe forcefully pushes Preacher off the porch and toward the barn. Preacher stumbles down the steps, but manages to stay on his feet.

"Now get in there and kill that son of a bitch." Munroe says.

"ALL OF YA." He yells.

"And make sure it sticks this time." Munroe adds.

Preacher, Emmett, Tenderfoot, Ty and red run toward the barn. Six Hatchet members are all that remain. For a man who doesn't like violence, Cole has racked up a pretty good body count in the last two days.

Inside the barn...

The five men enter through a side walk-in door and crouch behind stacked boxes. Preacher starts to pray in a low whisper. "The Lord is my Shepard, I shall fear no..."

Before preacher can finish his prayer, Ty slaps him in the back of the head. "Shut up. I don't wanna get killed on account of your bible spoutin'."

Preacher rubs the back of his head and gives Ty a mean look.

"You in here Cole?" Emmett asks.

Cole knows that Emmett is just trying to pinpoint his location. He answers anyway. "Yea I'm here ya murderin' bastard."

The five men look toward the stall that Cole's voice was coming from. Ty points at the stall, while looking at Emmett, Emmett nods his head. They know where he is now.

Cole Knows it don't matter anyway. What he is about to do would have giving his position away anyhow, but it might also rattle the Hatchet's nerves and that's why he's doing it. "Which one of you is called Red?" Cole asks.

Red looks at Emmett and Emmett nods his head at him. Red peeks over the crates he's hiding behind. "That would be me, what do..."

BANG! Before Red can finish his sentence, Cole puts a bullet right between his eyes. Red goes limp and falls over dead.

Cole was right it did rattle some nerves. The other four men quickly hunker down behind the crates. "Holy shit. He just killed Red." Ty says.

"That was for my daughter, ya son of a' bitch." Cole says.

Ty is the most scared and it shows. "We're sittin' ducks out here. He's gonna kill us all"

"NO HE AIN'T." Emmett yells, then tries to reassure Ty.

"Now get a' hold of your self Ty. He's only one man and there's still four of us left in here and the Colonel outside makes five."

Ty relaxes a bit and nods his head, realizing Emmett is right, they have Cole outnumbered.

"There was thirteen of us when we started." Tenderfoot says.

Ty realizing Tenderfoot is also right, gets a scared look on his face again and slides down to a seated position. Ty looks as though he is going to cry. "Oh shit, we're all gonna die."

"Damn it, Tenderfoot. What are ya trying ta do?" Emmett asks.

Tenderfoot just shrugs his shoulders and goes back to trying to see Cole.

"Buck up, Ty. We been in a lot worse scrapes than this. Now quit cowering and kill this pecker head sum bitch." Emmett says.

Ty nods, takes a deep breath, checks his revolver and slowly stands, pointing his revolver as he looks for Cole. Ty is so focused on not being scared that he doesn't realize how far up he is standing.

Just as Ty's chest rises above the crates, Cole

jumps from one stall to another fanning his Revolver. BANG! BANG! BANG! The first bullet strikes the crate in front of Ty. The next two bullets find their mark in Ty's chest. With a surprised look on his face, Ty looks at Emmett and then falls backward, dead.

"Hey, Preacher your next. Stand on up behind that bible and let me send your hypocrite ass ta hell." Cole says.

Preacher pulls his bible to his chest and holds it tight. "No gawd damn way." Preacher says.

In the back stall...

Cole is now in a squatted position with his back to one of the stall walls, he has the Remington Outlaw in his hand. "I'm gonna kill you Cole." Emmett says.

"Ya done tried once, I don't reckon you'll do much better this time around." Cole says.

Cole looks in the cylinder of the Remington Outlaw and turns it, it's empty. Cole Holsters the Remington Outlaw, reaches behind his back and grabs the Remington Frontier. He looks in the cylinder and rotates it, one bullet left. He reaches to feel his gun belts cartridge holders, nothing, no bullets. The bullets must have fallen out during the ruckus with Skinner. "Damn it." Cole whispers to himself.

He knows he should have checked his ammo this morning, but it's been along time sense he's had to do this much killing. Cole peeks around the edge of the wall towards the position of the Hatchet. Lined

130

up against the wall near the Hatchet's position Cole Spots the dynamite crates. He pulls his head back and leans against the stall wall once more. Cole knows he's got one bullet and one chance. It's a long shot, the crates could stop the bullet and he would waste his last shot. Even if the bullet penetrates the crate, that much dynamite could take the whole barn down and everything in it. Including not just the Hatchet, but Cole too.

Cole thinks that even if he doesn't survive, That without his men, Munroe would be less trouble for someone else. It's worth a shot, it's the only one he has.

Cole cocks the hammer on his revolver. He takes a deep breath and exhales. He leans out away from the wall and takes aim at the dynamite crates. "Here goes nuthin'." Cole says, as he takes another breath, holds it and squeezes the trigger.

Chapter 17
Dance With the Devil

Outside the barn...

Munroe is standing near by, with his revolver in hand. With a deafening sound the front quarter part of the barn explodes, sending boards and splinters flying in all directions. The force of the explosion knocks Munroe off his feet. His revolver flies out of his hand and lands in a mud puddle near a horse trough.

Munroe, still dazed, sets up to observe the damage. "God damn. What the hell was that?" Munroe says, knowing there's no one around to answer.

He hears a noise that sounds like wood being shoved around. Munroe looks toward the barn to see what it is.

Cole staggers out of the remains, his clothing is still smoldering and has smoke rolling off of them, he is still holding his revolver. Munroe scurries to quickly stand up. When he's on his feet he and Cole lock eyes. "Damn you Hawkins. You God damn rebel scum."

Cole is still staggering a bit from the explosion. "Yore the only one left, ya murderin' bastard." Cole says.

Cole raises his revolver, points it at Munroe and cocks the Hammer. Munroe gets a look of fear about him and holds his hands to the sides, palms facing Cole. "Come on Cole, let's talk this over."

Without saying a word Cole squeezes the trigger. CLICK! The revolver is empty. The explosion rattled him enough, that Cole forgot he shot the last bullet at the crates.

Munroe Smiles, reaches down and grabs a rifle off the ground. "You out of bullets Cole?"

Munroe levers the rifle and puts it to his shoulder and takes a slow, careful aim at Cole. "Here you can have one of mine."

Munroe squeezes the trigger. CLICK! Nothing he quickly levers the action again and Squeezes the trigger. CLICK! The rifles empty too.

Munroe throws the rifle down and pulls the tomahawk from his waist band. "Looks like we're gonna be doing this the hard way. Hell, it's only fittin' that us two old war horses go at it like this."

Then without warning, Munroe rushes toward Cole. Cole pulls his knife, in a saber grip, without having time to use the lanyard. Munroe slashes at

133

Cole's stomach. Cole hollows out, as the tomahawk blade cuts his shirt and grazes his skin, drawing blood. Cole reaches out and slashes at Munroe's face, nicking Munroe's cheek, Cole reverses directions and back hand slashes at Munroe's throat.

Munroe blocks the slash by slamming the tomahawk handle into Cole's arm, knocking Cole's knife from his hand. Munroe smiles and comes after Cole aggressively. He slashes at Cole's face with an inward slash then an outward slash. Cole is back peddling to keep from getting cut and Munroe is charging forward.

Munroe slashes inward at Cole's stomach, then outward, Cole shifting and dodging multiple slashes, winds up with his back against what's left of a barn wall. Munroe launches an overhead downward stroke toward Cole's face. Cole shifts his head narrowly avoiding the tomahawk as, it sticks deep into the side of the barn.

Cole quickly slams a punch into Munroe's Face. Munroe lets go of the tomahawk and stumbles backward. Cole rushes forward, grabs Munroe's collar with his left hand, and unloads four rapid punches into Munroe's face, with his right hand, WHAM, WHAM, WHAM, WHAM! Munroe starts to stagger, but before he can fall Cole kicks him backward and Munroe slams to the ground on his back.

"Yore times up Munroe, ya ain't gonna be able ta hurt anyone else." Cole says.

Munroe turns his head and spits blood on the ground and wipes his mouth with his sleeve. He looks around and spots a revolver under a piece of wood, next to himself. The revolver is turned just enough that he can see the bullet ends through the cylinder holes. It looks fully loaded.

"I ain't finished yet you rebel son of a bitch." Munroe says, as he grabs a handful of dirt and throws it at Cole's eyes, then grabs the revolver.

Cole quickly covers his eyes and staggers backward when the dirt hits his face. Munroe quickly jumps to his feet and checks the revolver, for bullets, just to be sure. He was right, it is fully loaded, Munroe smiles. "This one has beans in the wheel. Looks like it just ain't your day Hawkins."

Munroe now cocky, lowers the revolver to his side. Cole clears the dirt from his eyes looks over and sees he is standing next to the tomahawk, stuck in the barn.

"You ready to die?" Munroe asks.

Cole calmly reaches up and grips the handle of the tomahawk. Cole looks at Munroe with a confident look and asks, "How bout we bury the hatchet first?"

Munroe sees the tomahawk and laughs. "You really think you can yank that free, cover this distance and cut me down before I can put a bullet through your head?"

Cole is still calm and study. "Maybe. Maybe not. Let's find out." Cole says.

Cole has once again found himself in a position, where he has one chance, and yet again it is the only chance he has. All Cole needs is for Munroe to start rambling again, so that Cole can get a head start. All he needs is the element of surprise. He gets it.

Munroe starts to go into one of is ramblings.

"You called me crazy? Your the...."

Before Munroe can finish the statement, Cole jerks the tomahawk free and sprints hard toward Munroe. Munroe surprised by Cole's actions, slightly hesitates, then quickly raises the revolver, cocks the hammer and fires, BANG!

Chapter 18
The Pride of Lamont

The bullet pierces Cole's left arm but, Cole unfazed continues forward. Munroe re-cocks the revolver, but does not have time to fire a second shot. Cole buries the tomahawk deep into Munroe's skull and Munroe drops to the ground, it's over.

Cole has literally buried the Hatchet in more than one way. He's exhausted and dreads the chore of dragging Munroe's body back to find a horse, but it has to be done. People need to know that the Hatchets rein of terror is over and Munroe's body will prove it.

Later...

Cole rides back into Lamont from the east end of town. Bloody and battered, he is leading Munroe's horse with Munroe's body strapped over the saddle. Various towns people gather to look on in awe, Among them are Hanna, Billy, Sheriff Cooper, Dan, Cletus and Mr. Peavey.

Cole rides up to the Sheriff's office near Sheriff Cooper and stops. Both men stare at each other. Sheriff Cooper looks at Munroe strung over the saddle. Without saying a word Sheriff Cooper ducks his head, removes his badge and throws it on the ground. Still without a word, Boyd Cooper simply walks away, sheriff no more.

Billy runs over and picks up the badge and hands it to Cole. Cole takes the badge looks at it and replies. "This ain't mine boy."

Billy looks up proudly. "It ought ta be Mister Hawkins."

"What's yore name pard?" Cole asks.

"It's Billy, Billy Haskell, Sir."

Cole looks at Billy with a serious look on his face. "Well Billy Billy Haskell It's a pleasure ta meet ya."

Billy hesitates a bit not sure how to respond. "Uh thar's just one Billy Sir."

"I'm sure there is pard." Cole says

Cole knows that he's looking at a unique young man and that there can only be one Billy Haskell. "I was just teasin' ya Billy." Cole says as he smiles.

Billy gives a big smile right back. "It's a pleasure ta meet you too Sir."

Cole nods his head once to acknowledge Billy's statement, then holds the badge up. "Billy I appreciate the sentiment, but it's not yore decision ta make."

Billy nods, then ducks his head in disappointment. Mr. Peavey steps forward. "No it's not his decision but, it is ours."

Mr. Peavey looks around at the rest of the town folk. "Most of the members of the Merchants Association are here, so let's vote. Anyone apposed to Mister Hawkins becoming Sheriff speak now."

Everyone looks at each other but, no one speaks against the idea. "There you have it Mister Hawkins most everyone here wants you to be Sheriff. What do you say?" Mr. Peavey asks.

Cole looks at the badge then back at the town people. "Again, I appreciate the sentiment folks, but I ain't no lawman. Why don't one a' y'all wear this badge?" Cole asks.

Dan steps to the front. "You would make a better lawman than any of us, Mister Hawkins. I see all kinds come into my saloon and outlaws all over the country have known Lamont as a town without much of a lawman, for some time now. It's gonna take some doing to convince all the riffraff that comes through, that we got law now." Dan says.

"We don't just need someone to wear a badge Mister Hawkins, we need someone who can back it up. We need you Mister Hawkins." Dan finishes.

Everyone nods in agreement and once again Cole looks at the badge, then back at the people. Hanna steps forward. Hanna resented Cole the first time she saw him. That's changed now. She now realizes that this town will not survive without a man like Cole Hawkins to protect it. "Mister Hawkins this town needs someone who is willing and able to do what needs doing to bring law and order back."

Cletus steps forward, to add his two bits. "Yore the only one can do it Mister Hawkins."

"The lot of ya are makin' me feel mighty old callin' me Mister Hawkins all the time." Cole says.

"Someone want ta take care of this body?" Cole asks.

Everyone looks disappointed. They think Cole has dismissed the offer and is now trying to change the subject.

"Yes sir, I'll take care of it." Cletus says.

Cletus takes the reins of Munroe's horse.

"This town have a Doc?" Cole asks.

"Yes sir." Cletus responds.

"Ya might aught ta fetch em', I reckon I'm gonna need some patchin'." Cole says.

"Yes sir. I'll get em'." Cletus says, still disappointed.

"Can somebody take care of my horse?" Cole asks.

"Yes sir. I'll take care of that too." Cletus says, as he takes hold of Cole's reins.

Cole eases out of the saddle, with pain, then looks back at Cletus. "Thank ya. Yore a' good man." Cole looks at the sheriff's office. "The sheriff's office have sleepin' quarters?"

"Yes sir." Cletus says.

"Good." Cole says, as he pins on the badge and scans the crowd.

"Well, I reckon if anyone needs me I'll be in my office."

Cole heads for the door of the sheriff's office. Pleased with Cole's decision, everyone smiles and Cletus nods excitedly. "Yes sir Sheriff. You don't worry bout nuthin', I'll take care of everything. Sheriff Hawkins."

With that statement Cole stops and turns around. He smiles at Cletus and nods, then heads into the sheriff's office. Cole is still unsure about the decision. But there's something about *Sheriff Hawkins*, that has a ring to it. Cole thinks somehow it sounds good, it sounds right.

Hanna looks down at Billy, who is smiling as big as he can. "What do you think now, Billy?" Hanna asks.

"I think ya were right, Miss Jenkins, things are gonna get better. I also think I'm gonna be proud ta live in this town."

Hanna smiles, puts her arm around Billy and pulls him close. "I think we all are, Billy. Everyone of us."

This town can now regain it's pride. When Cole started out he never new he would be the pride of Lamont. The Hatchet are dead and no longer a threat, but this town is not out of danger yet. There will be outlaws and bandits who will try and get a foot hold here sooner or later. But with decent folk who live here and the help of Cole Hawkins, Lamont stands a good chance.

Sometimes that's all that decent people need, is a chance. Let the outlaws and bandits come. They will no longer find an easy target. You know how the saying goes. "They better look out, cause there's a new sheriff in town."

THE END
or a new beginning?

AMMON E PROLIFE

PATH

OF THE

SOUL

THE FINAL JOURNEY